Just Jake
SHIRLEY LARSON

Harlequin Books

TORONTO • NEW YORK • LONDON
AMSTERDAM • PARIS • SYDNEY • HAMBURG
STOCKHOLM • ATHENS • TOKYO • MILAN

Published September 1990

ISBN 0-373-25414-8

Printed in U.S.A.

"I don't like your caveman techniques," she protested

Alexandra wriggled against the softness of the pillows in a futile attempt to escape Jake, but his grip on her was unyielding. "What do you want?" she asked, looking mischievous.

Jake eased his weight away, slightly releasing his hold. "I want you to say, *Jake is my lover.*" They had played that game when they were children—his demanding she say what he decreed, but never quite like this....

Her eyes met his and a sensuous smile curved her lips. "You're being ridiculous—"

"Say it, Alex," Jake whispered, caressing her gently, coaxing her to say the words.

Alexandra felt herself losing control . . . and losing the game. But when Jake shifted on top of her, winning no longer mattered. Her need for him was suddenly overpowering. "You're my lover, Jake," she cried out. "My love...."

Shirley Larson has written more than twenty novels in her long and prolific career. *Just Jake*, the story of a dedicated pediatrician and an up-and-coming Realtor, was first inspired by a trip the author took to the Florida Keys. Shirley wanted to explore the popular fantasy of a woman who could be *completely* loved, no matter what professional considerations her lover had. And as a busy romance writer, Shirley can well identify with people devoted to their careers!

Books by Shirley Larson

1

HE WAS gaining on her.

Alexandra Holden took a deep breath, tried to hang loose and pushed herself to jog faster over the sandy beach. Just once in her life she'd like to beat Jake Hustead in a footrace.

Behind her the Florida sunshine glowed golden. The ocean slapped against the Duck Key beach with a pure, clean sound, and the air sparkled with crisp early-morning coolness. This was her favorite time—the precious hour of solitude she needed to think about her day and organize herself before she went to the office.

Still have those notes to go over before the staff meeting. The calls about the gallery opening—when to do those? Four o'clock—just before Sarah goes home. I'll divide the list with her alphabetically. No, that won't work. If I don't call Lealda personally, she won't come...

Behind her Jake pounded the sand in a rhythmic stride that was out of sync with the slap of her running shoes. He was six-two to her five-six and he had a longer stride.

"You're on my beach," she said, when he pulled up next to her.

"You always were a territorial little—"

"Ah, ah, ah. No judgmental name-calling allowed before eight o'clock in the morning on Thursdays. Besides, you're the one who taught me to be territorial. You were always crawling over onto my half of the playpen."

"Well, how do you think I felt, being locked in a cage with a good-looking female, when I was too much of a baby to do anything about it?"

"Character-building, Doctor, character-building. And see? It worked. You're definitely a character..."

He reached out to grab her shoulder. She extended her stride just enough to elude him. They laughed and ran on side by side.

Jake looked comfortable, easy in his body. He was thirty-five, only three months older than her, and, like her, he'd always enjoyed physical exercise. His tank top and shorts revealed a body that was lithe and lean, almost as bronzed as a native's. In the two weeks since he'd moved his practice from New York State to the Florida Keys, he'd lost his northern pallor. His throat, arms and legs were golden brown and his coffee-brown hair showed subtle sun streaks.

He turned his head and smiled at her. He'd always had an endearing smile, even more so now with those lines mature men get around their mouths and eyes. He might have made nice company too, if it wasn't for his eyes. Those green eyes of his could eat a woman alive— and make her glad to be his meal.

She felt a sudden little shiver of anticipation, as if she'd just met an intriguing new man. Impossible. He was just...Jake. "You were precocious, but you weren't that advanced. You might try to fool another unsuspecting female into thinking you went straight from diapers to macho, but not me. I was there, remember?"

"Welcome home, Jake," he murmured. "I can always depend on you to keep me humble."

Suddenly she felt foolish. Jake had moved in next door to her just two weeks ago, and already she was at him. An old habit. Self-defense. Attack or be attacked. Surely it was time to cease hostilities. After all, they were both adults.

She stopped running, turned and held out her hand. "I really am glad you're here. It'll be good to have you around again."

He clasped her hand, his eyes bright with an emotion she couldn't identify. "Sincere, adult, polite. Coming from you, I'm not sure I can handle those weird grown-up qualities."

She cocked her head as if thinking about it. "Try being honest, straightforward." Her eyes brightened and her mouth tilted. "And respectful."

"Respectful?" He grinned, showing a flash of white teeth in his tanned face. "You ask too much."

"Well, try." His hand felt too warm, too big on hers. Feeling consumed with heat, she pulled away from him.

Suddenly, surprisingly, Jake sat down on the sand and started taking off his shoes.

"What are you doing?" she asked him.

"Going for a dip."

"Should I turn around? How much are you going to take off?"

"Don't get too excited." Easily, gracefully, still clothed in his swim trunks and tank top, he stood. "Are you coming in?"

She shook her head. "Mother told me never to go swimming with guys who keep their clothes on."

"No guts, no glory."

Typical, Alexandra thought, watching him. Wading in full blast, enjoying every sensation, without a particle of fear or hesitancy. Alive. Vibrantly alive. He always had been.

Watching him made her feel the same way. The sun seemed brighter, the air softer, the water cooler.

He turned and splashed backward, and then, like a child, sat down on his rear end in the water. No standing on ceremony for Jake. Her mouth curled in a smile. When he was fifteen, she recalled, he'd tried to stand up on the roller coaster, and she'd pulled him back down into his seat. He'd said he wanted to see what it would feel like. She'd found out later the idiot had made a bet with Sean Harding. She'd pulled Jake back too soon and he hadn't collected. He'd been angry with her for a week. She'd been just as angry with him for being so reckless.

He wasn't in danger today. The water was shallow for several feet out, and the surf, like most places in the Keys, was gentle. Although she knew he didn't need a guardian, she felt strangely compelled to stand there and watch him play.

He came up out of the water pushing his hair back, communing with the ocean, celebrating the water with a primitive abandon that reflected his unique personality. Jake worked hard, played hard, knew what he wanted and went after it, whether it was a swim in the ocean, a medical career, or a woman.

He was a successful pediatrician, but he hadn't been as fortunate with his women. How long had he been separated from Kim? It had to be about a year and a half, almost the same amount of time she and Clay had been divorced. Did he have scars? He probably did. Who didn't at their age? She had a few herself.

Suddenly she felt she wanted to share them with him, heal them with him.

Jake stood up in the water and turned toward her. A ray of sunshine slanted off his face, sheening his profile, turning his skin to a liquid gold that flowed over his facial bones, outlining the sleek blade of his nose.

There was tremendous power in his face—power that was centered, refined, and heightened in his eyes.

He knew she was thinking about him.

He might have changed in other ways, but he hadn't lost the knack of reading her mind. He'd always had that, ever since they were children. She'd been both drawn to and repelled by his ability to understand her.

As if he sensed her drawing back, he turned away from her toward the dawn, bathed in the light, standing like a primitive man making obeisance to the rising sun. "Look at it, Alex."

Her eyes shifted away from his masterful figure to the sky beyond. She'd never seen a gold sky before, not until this moment. She'd never felt the effect of dawn like this before—under her skin, down to her bones where it sizzled, melting all the heartache she'd ever had. She wanted this moment to be eternal. She wanted to experience this incredible awareness, this communion with the world forever.

Just when she felt most vulnerable, he turned back to her and held out his hand. "Come and play, Alex."

He read her heart's secrets in her face. Just as he always had been able to.

With his wet hair slicked back from his face, he was more tempting than the devil himself. His eyes, as hypnotic and inviting as the sea, ordered her to forget her sense of time, forget her work, forget her life.

"Come and play, Alex," he repeated. There was command in his tone, seriousness in his face. The dark invitation to obey was almost irresistible.

"I'm sorry, Jake. I...can't." She knew she had to suit action to words. She had to turn her back to him and jog back to her house. As fast as she could. Back to reality. Yet, she didn't move. She stood very still, watching him.

He reached toward her, grasped her shoulder.

She wrenched loose and backed away. He stalked her from the side, forcing her to shift around, her back to the ocean.

"Say you're scared of me," he ordered, smiling, playing the old game. "Say you're scared, or you're going for a swim."

It was a game they'd played often as kids. He would advance, his face full of mock threat in his attempt to frighten her—she would retreat, all the while pretending to be brave, strong, and unmoved by his threats.

She was no longer a child. "Jake, stop it. This is ridiculous. You can't frighten me. You never could." She was very serious, very dignified. When she thought she'd distracted him, she feinted to the left.

He was too quick for her. Shaking his head at her as if he was very disappointed in her little ploy, he dragged her backward into the water, his face serious, his hand firmly gripping her arm.

"You're ruining my forty-nine dollar Reeboks," she complained, as the water swirled around her ankles and spilled into her sneakers.

"I'll buy you new ones."

"Jake, stop it," she protested, but she had a silly urge to smile. The water was cool and silky on her legs, and she felt like a kid playing truant, strangely light and relieved of responsibility. She realized her hands weren't working very hard at pushing him away. "I've got to go home to get ready for work—"

"That's a four letter word I can't allow you to use in my ocean." He shook his head as if she'd made a grave error. "You shouldn't say it. You shouldn't even think it." He smiled pleasantly and put both hands on her shoulders. "Do you remember that time at the lake when you got Denny Evans to pay you two dollars if you pushed me off the dock? What a budding little entrepreneur you were, getting Evans to pay you for doing something you already wanted to do."

"You were totally obnoxious that summer," she said. "You were showing off for your new girlfriend and you deserved that dunking..."

"I never got even with you for that, did I?" His smile deepened. He pushed her toward the ocean while she resisted. To no avail. He force-marched her backward, taking her in deeper and deeper. The water crept up over her knees, her thighs, her hips. In no time, she was submerged to her shoulders.

Thinking quickly, she wrenched herself free of his hold and splashed back in the water. She stumbled upright, gasping, as if she'd swallowed too much water. She deliberately lost her footing, coughed as if she'd breathed a half-gallon of water into her lungs and splashed forward onto her stomach into a dead man's float, letting her limbs go slack. She realized her chances of fooling Jake into thinking she'd passed out and was seconds away from drowning were almost nil, but she had to try.

He said something in a dryly mocking tone, but she couldn't make out the words.

She stayed as still as she could, letting the undulating motion of the waves rock her body. Her clothes clung to her thighs. Her shoes were waterlogged and heavy, and she had to fight to keep her feet afloat. Her breath burned in her lungs. She was quickly running out of air.

Time seemed to stretch endlessly. The water sloshed over her. If she could wait a little longer, maybe this time she could fool him . . .

The world spun and her body screamed with the need to breathe. She lunged upright, gasping for air.

Jake stood at a distance, his arms folded, his green eyes coolly mocking. The water she'd disturbed swirled around his thighs. "You're an idiot."

She glared at him, her eyes flashing silver fire. "Why is it I can never fool you?" Her hair was a mess. Water poured from her shorts down her thighs.

His gaze was like the ocean—dark and deep. An odd tension hovered. She felt as if he was touching her face with that dark, intense look.

"Maybe because I know you better than you know yourself," he replied softly.

She felt awkward, transparent. The way she'd always felt with him. And now there was a new element added to the power he had over her. She was terribly aware of Jake's body—his fingers lying against the bulge of his biceps in his folded arms, the wet hair on his chest, the strength of his shoulders, the narrowness of his waist, the evidence of his maleness between his thighs.

She was looking at Jake and thinking about sex.

The thought was so disturbing that her knees wobbled. She reached out for support and found her hands clasping Jake lightly at the waist.

A sparkle of sunlight flared in his eyes. Could he read her mind now?

"I'm sorry," she said and moved to pull her hands away. He unfolded his arms just enough to squeeze his elbows to his body and trap her fingers there.

"Apologizing for touching me is a little too adult and civil," he said, his voice as dark as his eyes.

Caught in the awkwardness of the moment, she slipped her hands away from his damp, warm sides and took a step back from him. Too late she realized her wet clothes were as revealing as his. He was looking at her intently, awareness trapped in the green depths of his eyes like a reflecting pool, taking her in. Consuming her. She had to turn away.

This couldn't be happening. She couldn't allow herself to feel like a woman with him. He was just . . . Jake. "I've got to get back."

"Yes, of course."

When she turned to retrace her path to the house, Jake fell into step beside her.

The silence was too long, too potent. Alexandra sought for a way to break it, but it was Jake who said, "Remember that winter our families came down here together and you got sick because you'd eaten so much key lime pie?"

She took up the challenge instantly. "Only because you dared me to eat that fourth piece."

"You were such a—"

"Glutton for punishment, yes, I know. You repeat that corny tag every time you tell that story. And you've been telling it since we were sixteen." She walked along at his side, scuffing her soaked and sand-covered sneakers on the hard-packed beach, oddly grateful to him for relaxing the tension between them.

"Were you ever sorry your dad sold out his real estate business up North and moved down here?" he asked.

"No." That was not the exact truth, but it was as much as she wanted to share.

"It must have been tough on you, being a teenager and having to leave all your friends."

It had been tough, but she didn't want to admit it to Jake. The toughest thing had been realizing, too late, what a large part of her life he'd been. "What about you?" she asked, "did you hate it that your dad stayed in New York State?"

"No." He stared off into the sunrise. "I was old enough to realize his medical practice was too big for him to pick up and move as easily as your dad could move his business. I was always glad our mothers stayed in touch. I've never thanked Beatrice properly for being so good to my mother after my father died. I don't know what I would have done with Mom if Beatrice hadn't been there to help her."

"No thanks necessary. My mother had been through it all, so she knew how yours was feeling. We were glad when she moved down here next to us. Your mother's a sweetheart." She slanted him a devilish glance. "Sure blows the theory that heredity and environment play the biggest part in influencing a person's character, doesn't it?"

"You're asking for it, Holden." They were back on familiar ground, teasing each other unmercifully.

Unwilling to explore the implications of his comment, she reverted to conventional conversation. "What made you decide to move your practice down here, Jake?"

"A combination of things, I guess. Turning thirty-five, thinking maybe my mother wasn't getting any younger, and a need to—see some new scenery."

They were nearly at the house. "I'm sorry things didn't work out between you and Kim," she said.

"Don't be. We're better off apart than we were together."

She decided to let that go by without comment. She'd met Kim once and hadn't liked her, but that didn't keep her from wishing that Jake would find a woman worthy of him, and find marital bliss. She wanted him to be happy. She always had.

She turned to continue walking toward the house and he followed her. "Things didn't work out too well for you in the matrimonial department, either, did they?" he asked.

"Not too well, no." She turned to look at him with eyes that were honest and clear. "With all the insight you and my brother gave me on the male sex, you'd think I'd be a whiz at keeping a marriage together, wouldn't you?"

"Don't take all the blame, Alex. It takes two to keep the ship of matrimony afloat."

The tone of his voice did strange things to her, made nerves tighten that she thought had atrophied. She felt totally understood, totally accepted, totally *loved*. The nervousness came flooding back, bringing with it the feeling of raw vulnerability.

"Are you getting used to Florida living?"

"Well, I have to admit it was a little tough at first," his drawl lengthened, "the constant sunshine, the warmth, the vista of sea outside my office door, the do-it-mañana attitude of the natives. But I persevered and I adjusted. It took me all of—" he frowned, considering "—ten minutes."

She rapped a clenched fist lightly on his shoulder. He retaliated in kind. She shook her head and smiled at him. "I'd like to go on exchanging blows with you, Hustead, but *I'm* not a favored member of the medical profession. This isn't my day off."

"Pity," he murmured.

Jake was looking at her oddly, like the Great Stone Face with only his eyes showing the fire of life. She smoothed her wet hair back from her face. "What's the matter with you? Did you swallow too much sea water?"

He gave her a sardonic glance, as if she ought to know better. "Yeah, something like that."

She realized she was staring at him again and she knew she had to stop. He looked sleek when he was wet, like a jaguar slicked down after a run, a male animal honed to fine lines of pure masculinity. Heaven to touch, hell to cage.

"You'd better go in and change before the beach bunnies come out into the noonday sun. They'll think you're something left over from another planet."

It was an outright lie, but Jake didn't seem to notice. He smiled and the strange tension gripping Alexandra vanished. In a gentlemanly manner, he clicked the soggy heels of his sneakers together. "You do know how to keep a man humble, my lady."

"I practiced on you every chance I got."

"And loved every minute of it," he murmured.

"Hey, don't knock it. I kept you from being a conceited, overbearing, spoiled, only child."

"I admit to having had a tiny measure of conceit, and a touch of overbearing. But spoiled child, never."

"Race you to the house," she challenged him.

"Loser buys Sunday's pizza?"

"You're on."

He let her win, but pretended he hadn't. They agreed on pepperoni with mushrooms. She reminded him he'd have to buy enough for the five of them—his mother, her mother, and her niece, as well as the two of them. He'd have a regular harem. Could he count that high, she'd asked teasingly. Maybe he'd have to pretend he was a pasha, counting his women. He drawled that he was capable of counting as long as the number didn't go higher than he had fingers, and he might make a passable pasha . . . with a little practice.

She laughed and turned to leave him, the sound of her laughter echoing in his ears.

ON HIS MOTHER'S PATIO, Jake kicked off one wet sneaker, then the other, making little showers of sand fly and leaving them where they lay. His feet sandy and bare, he bounded up the steps to the sliding glass door that led into the white-carpeted living room. The quiet within told him his mother was still asleep.

He went into the bathroom, shed his wet clothes and stepped into the stinging cold of the shower. He lathered his hairy chest vigorously, thinking about the luxury of the day off that lay ahead of him. Then he wondered what he was going to do with it.

An hour later, after he'd showered, shaved and had breakfast with Helen, his mother, he drove down the Overseas Highway toward Marathon. He had some vague idea of chartering one of the dozens of deep-sea fishing boats that bumped against the dock there. Deep-sea fishing was one of the attractions that had brought him to the Keys. But for some reason, he wasn't in the mood to go fishing with strangers.

He had a sudden vision of sun-kissed hair blowing in the breeze and a teasing smile. He wanted to go with someone he could talk and laugh with, someone who would enjoy the sea and the sun as much as he did. Someone like Alex. But Alex wasn't available.

At the side of the road, an old cowboy hawked airplane rides over the Keys. Twenty bucks, the sign said. Shades of the old barnstormer days. On impulse, Jake swung his car onto the side road.

The cowboy, lean and lanky as a pull of beef jerky and almost as brown, came walking up to the car with a studied smile. He tipped back his broad-brimmed hat with a wrinkled finger. "Howdy. Nice day we're having today. Beautiful weather for flying. Care to take a spin?"

"How long is the ride?"

"Twenty minutes. He'll fly you out to the reef and back."

Out to the reef and back sounded good to Jake. He rolled forward in his seat to take his billfold from his pocket, and the cowboy's mouth lifted in a genuine grin.

A man and woman and their small son pulled up just as Jake was climbing out of his car. There were two planes and two pilots; one would take the family up, the other would take Jake up in the little brown-striped Cessna. When Jake walked through the gate toward the plane, he heard the cowboy breaking into a chorus of "Blueberry Hill." The little boy was staring up at him with big eyes. Jake's mouth curled in a smile.

After the plane lifted off the runway, the pilot gave him a running commentary which Jake only half listened to. He was looking down at the Keys, thinking the pieces of land jutting up in the water were burdened down with buildings like too many raisins on top of a sticky bun. The Keys were losing their World War II look and were coming of age. Maybe too fast. And Alex was helping speed their development.

At the end of one promontory stood a high-rise building, nine stories high. Alex's building. Her office was there, at the top. Holden Real Estate. She'd been twenty-five when her father had died and she'd taken it over from him. In ten years, she'd doubled the size of the company. One successful lady executive. She didn't look her age, but she'd be thirty-five in June.

His thoughts wandered back to their morning encounter—the way she looked with her blond-brown hair blown forward around her head by the sea breeze, the stubborn little tilt of her jaw, her clothes wet and clinging to a body that was slim but rounded with good hips and a nice rear end. All woman. Had he ever really looked at Alex before this morning? Hell, yes, he'd looked plenty when he was sixteen. He remembered that summer with sudden, vivid awareness. He remembered seeing Alex in a bikini and the shame and frustration he felt at his inability to control his body when he looked at her. He'd been awkward and wild and a little crazy. He'd retaliated by making a damned nuisance of himself, showing off for Marian Rogers. No wonder Alex had shoved him off the dock. He'd nearly made her hate him that summer. It was only later he'd understood why he'd acted the way he had. They'd been too close. Instinctively, he'd driven her away. The alternative was to get much more intimate.

But he'd known he couldn't do that. Their families had been friends for too long. The whole time they were growing up, the Holdens and the Husteads had lived beside each other in a small town in upstate New York. When it came time to take winter vacations, the families had crammed children, suitcases and one small poodle—his mother's—into a van and driven to Florida to find warmth and sunshine. When he and Alex were fifteen, the cold weather on the mainland of Florida had forced them to drive farther south to the Keys. A year later, Adam Holden had sold out his business in New York State and moved his family to Duck Key. Jake had told himself he was glad. But when the Holden van rolled out of the driveway for the last time, he found himself clenching his fists until his nails bit into his palms.

The women had stayed in touch. There had been holiday reunions over the years and the Husteads had vacationed with the Holdens for a few weeks during the winter months. The adults maintained their friendship, but for the two teenagers, time, distance, different schools and different friends had made them strangers. The old rapport was gone. He'd felt awkward with her on the few days a year he saw her, and he was pretty sure she felt just the same.

Today though, he hadn't felt awkward with her. He'd felt alive, real, ready—for what? To start over again—to recreate the old intimacy? Impossible.

The plane soared over the reef. Jake looked down at the silky green water mottled by the dark shadows. Coral lay hidden below the surface, its sharp edges waiting to snag some unsuspecting boater. He thought of Alex and the shadows that lurked under the surface of her silvery eyes—a consequence of the hurt she'd experienced over the years.

He'd never liked her ex-husband, Clay. He remembered a recent Christmas that had left a bitter taste in his mouth—the Christmas he'd walked into his mother's house and discovered that Alex, her new husband Clay and her mother had flown north to spend Christmas with the Husteads. He'd thought Clay self-serving and facile, and he was amazed that Alex had picked him to spend the rest of her life with. Then, Alex's brother and his wife were killed in a plane crash in Alaska, and she'd taken in their daughter. Jake reckoned that Alex's ambitious young husband, who had his eye on a senatorial seat and wanted her with him on the campaign trail, was too selfish to share his home with a young girl who wasn't his daughter, or to acknowledge the fact that Katherine might need Alex to stay at home with her.

Alex was a perfectionist. She didn't like to fail. But after her broken marriage, she'd picked up her life and gone on. She was immersed in her work. He knew, from his mother's account, that Alex worked long hours, made a lot of money, and was doing well. There was no reason to worry about her—and no reason to think she might need him.

Looking down he saw two highways threading out from Marathon over the water, a new one running beside the old one built after World War II. Locked in parallel paths but never touching. Like Alex's life and his. The old nameless feeling seized him—the feeling of wanting something he couldn't have.

"Seen all you want to see?" the pilot asked Jake.

"Yeah," said Jake.

"I'll take you back down to terra firma."

"You do that."

DURING THE LATE AFTERNOON, on the top floor of that nine-story building Jake had looked at, Alexandra was having trouble keeping her mind on the business at hand. She kept thinking of that golden sunrise and the cool silkiness of the ocean on her body. And the warmth of Jake's hands.

It was too easy to sit in her executive chair at the head of the conference table and, in the middle of her staff meeting, conjure up visions of those brilliant eyes and that lazy smile. Because they were discussing the rental of his office space, Jake's name was the third word out of everybody's mouth.

Bruce Dugan sat drumming the table with his pencil eraser in a rock rhythm, heavy accents alternating with light. "We should give him notice as soon as possible," was his uncompromising opinion.

Lea Kettavong's lips lifted in a slight smile, her dark eyes reflecting her tolerant amusement, her Asian beauty undimmed by a long day's work. In a soft voice she suggested that it would do no harm to delay the final decision until they'd examined all the options.

There was no question about Sarah Washington's opinion. Beautifully made-up, impeccably dressed in a gray business suit that had been especially tailored to fit her tall slim frame, the black woman, who was Alexandra Holden's personal assistant, was in favor of immediate eviction.

Sarah's eyes met Alexandra's across the table. "Putting off making a decision isn't going to change anything. The fact remains that we can't afford to refuse the developer's offer for that beach property simply because of an old verbal promise."

Alexandra made a restless movement with her hands. "There must be another solution. Come on, people, I need ideas. Maybe there's a different way to handle it."

Sarah's dark eyes gazed at her coolly. "Are you looking for another solution because Dr. Hustead has refused to move . . . or because you don't want to tell him he has to move so soon after his arrival?"

Alexandra met Sarah's penetrating gaze head on. "'B,'" she answered just as coolly.

Sarah's eyes flickered away. "I understand your unwillingness to go back on an old promise. But there is no other solution. You must tell the good doctor he's got to look for other premises. The sooner you do so, the better it will be for him."

"And for us?" An eyebrow arched delicately on Alexandra's forehead.

"And for us," Sarah echoed uncompromisingly. She hesitated and her voice softened. "Even though your father—and you—did promise his family lifetime use of that house on the beach."

Alexandra got to her feet and paced to the window. Never-never land hour in the Sunshine State. The traffic was tied up on the Overseas Highway as usual because of construction. Was Jake out in the bumper-to-bumper traffic enjoying his day off, unaware that she was considering telling him he'd have to move out of his office before he even got nicely settled in?

She turned away from the window. "I'd like to table it for another two weeks. In the meantime, if anybody comes up with any ideas, I'd appreciate hearing them. That's all I have. It's time you people went home."

They weren't about to argue with that. They began to leave, Bruce stowing away pencil and eraser, Lea rising gracefully, Sarah stuffing her papers into her briefcase. She was too good a businesswoman to show her disapproval, but Alexandra could read the signs of it in the angle of her shoulders. *This delay isn't helping anything*, those shoulders said.

The others left, Sarah lingered. Her briefcase in her hand, she propped it on the table.

"You're only postponing the inevitable."

Alexandra lifted her chin. "Maybe it only seems inevitable."

"You're not facing the facts."

"I'm facing the facts we have. I'm just looking for other ones."

"You've known Dr. Hustead for a long time?" The query was polite, an opening. Alexandra would bet that Sarah knew to the day how long the Holdens had known the Husteads.

"We crawled around in the same playpen."

Sarah was quiet for a moment, her gaze thoughtful. "You could have avoided the whole problem by telling him you were thinking of selling his property before he moved down here," she said finally.

Silvery eyes flashed over her. "I'm aware of that."

"Are you aware of your reasons for not telling him? If you had given him advance notice," Sarah went on relentlessly, "he might have changed his mind about coming, isn't that true?"

"If Dr. Hustead had changed his plans, it wouldn't have concerned me—"

"Wouldn't it?" Sarah didn't wait for an answer. Her dark eyes deep with a woman's knowledge, she picked up her briefcase and walked to the door.

"Sarah?"

Her hand on the knob, Sarah turned back to look at Alexandra.

She wanted to deny the truth of Sarah's words, wanted to say, *of course you're wrong.* But she would be lying if she did. "Be careful driving home." Her mouth curved in a smile. "It's a jungle out there."

2

It was a measure of Jake's supreme welcome in the Holden house that he was permitted to lounge on the couch with his feet on the coffee table. He'd taken off his shoes, of course; still, no one but Jake was allowed to use Beatrice's genuine cherry Queen Anne table for a footstool. Beatrice Holden was blatantly prejudiced in Jake's favor.

Sunday night was Alex's favorite time. Katherine, her niece, always seemed to relax more when they ate their supper in front of the TV set. Alex cast worried eyes over the twelve-year-old girl. She was going back into her shell again, the way she always did when there was someone in the house she didn't know very well.

She didn't know Jake. She'd met him two Christmases ago, the first year she'd been with Alexandra, and she'd seen him a few times since then, but despite Jake's natural way with young people, Katherine hadn't warmed to him. She still bore the scars of the sudden loss of both mother and father in that plane crash in Alaska. Since then, she seemed unable to care deeply about anything. She'd been confused and shocked and she'd had difficulty adjusting to the change in school, friends, climate. Alex wasn't sure she'd ever adjusted to her new life.

Jake's medical practice specialized in children. He was well aware of the silent fears, the unspoken grief and worries some children carried with them. He'd made a few friendly overtures, but when Katherine didn't respond, he hadn't pushed.

Now he seemed supremely at home in this room full of females. Beatrice and Helen sat in chairs set back from the TV set so they could talk. Jake lounged on the couch beside Alex, while Katherine was across the room seated on the floor with her back propped up against an easy chair.

Jake finished his pizza, polished off his glass of beer, relaxed back against the couch cushions and closed his eyes. "So what are you going to do about my lease, Alex?"

Alex's relaxed mood vanished. Aggravated, she glanced over at him. She'd found the courage to explain the situation to him while they'd been eating. He'd listened but he hadn't said much. Wasn't it just like him to get all comfy and cozy, then toss the bomb back at her? "I don't know." She took a deep breath and laid down the crust of pizza she'd been trying to convince herself she shouldn't eat, but knew she was going to anyway. "The offer on that property is a good one."

"Why didn't you tell me about it when I called you six months ago?"

Her mouth tightened. "Because the offer wasn't firm then."

"And when you did get it, you thought it would be better to let me go ahead and move in before you gave me the bad news."

"I thought it would be better if you came down here and got established first. Then, if we decided to sell, you could look around while you were already down here. It would be easier to find another place."

He sat up and looked at her. "I'm ready to find another place now."

His voice was smooth and calm though cold. "Just say the word, Alex. Don't keep me on tenterhooks wondering what you're going to do."

"Aunt Alex, would you excuse me?"

Alexandra pulled her attention away from Jake and gazed at Katherine, seeing the flush in her cheeks. She'd barely eaten half a piece of pizza. "Honey, I'm sorry. Were we talking too loud for you to hear the TV?"

"No, I just don't care to watch anymore. I thought I'd go out for a walk on the beach. May I?"

"Yes, of course you can go."

The girl scrambled to her feet and left the room quietly, far too quietly.

When Alex's puzzled eyes returned to Jake's face, he gestured at the television set and said, "They were talking about death."

"On a sitcom?"

He shrugged. "Some ditsy character was going on about how nothing matters in the end, we're all going to die anyway."

Alex muttered an unladylike word.

"Exactly my sentiments. Has she opened up to you much?"

"No. She hasn't opened up at all. She keeps everything locked up inside. I thought it was better to give her time, but—"

"Care to let me try?"

"Go right ahead. I'll take any help I can get, especially from an expert in the field."

"I was thinking about kite flying. Remember what fun we used to have on that hill above the lake?"

"I remember."

"I think I'll go home and dig that old kite out of my stuff."

Loose-limbed, amazingly agile for his height, Jake rose from the couch, stuck his feet into his shoes and ambled out the door.

ON THE BEACH, he caught sight of Katherine walking along the edge of the ocean with the listlessness that only the young can communicate when they're bored or unhappy. He wondered at his own audacity. Who did he think he was, plunging in to solve Alex's problems? After all, he might make things worse. The thought gave him pause. He dropped down on the sand and kicked off the sneakers he'd donned so hastily in Beatrice's living room, peeling off his socks and rolling up the bottoms of his jeans. Then he stood up, took a breath and, kite in hand, loped up behind Katherine.

"Mind if I walk along with you?"

She turned to look at him, her dark eyes faintly startled. The surprise vanished and the perpetual look of guardedness returned. She was an intelligent girl. She could easily figure out he wasn't out for a casual walk. In one cool look she'd taken in his Huck Finn disguise and she wasn't buying it, not a bit of it. But she couldn't do what she obviously wanted to do and tell him to go fly his kite some other place. That would have shown emotion . . . and caring. "Suit yourself."

Jake had skied on a subarctic mountaintop where the air was warmer than it was around Miss Katherine Holden, but he too had his own streak of stubbornness. He unreeled the kite, getting it aloft on the second try. The plastic rattled in the breeze. At least something was making a noise. "You want to hold it?"

"No."

Brilliant try, Ace. Now what are you going to do? He didn't know. He only knew he was into it now and he couldn't back out. "Why not?" he said, trying to sound casual, but feeling like a jackass.

She turned to look at him with eyes that seemed a hundred years old. "If I took hold of the string, that kite would fall down and break. Like right now."

Her conviction that she would destroy anything she touched jolted Jake. He hadn't expected it. He'd expected grief or anger, not a colossal load of guilt. He wasn't sure he was capable of lifting such a heavy load from her young back. "Sure about that?" he heard himself saying inanely.

"Positive."

Now what? He searched his mind frantically for a reply. Casual. Keep things casual. She isn't going to accept any Polyanna philosophizing from you. Specifics. He needed to deal in specifics. "Too bad. You're going to miss out on a lot of things in life if you don't touch something because you're afraid you may break it. The feel of exquisite glass, the stickiness of candy, the hand of another human being . . ." He stared up at the kite, wishing he could just shake the daylights out of her, wishing he could tell her she was lucky, damn lucky to have Alex care about her.

"Not wanting to break things isn't a crime. There's nothing wrong with me."

So much for his attempt at child psychology. "Of course there's nothing wrong with you. You just happen to be a little angry around the edges, that's all."

That got her attention. Her eyes flashed as she turned to him. "And that's all wrong, right?"

"No, it's exactly right." He smiled at her and wished he'd paid more attention in the one psychology class he'd taken. It obviously wasn't his strong suit. He did remember something about anger and guilt being emotions that came in the same bushel basket with grief. And that the best way to deal with a grieving person was to do so honestly. From the heart. "If I were you, I'd be angry, too. Probably a lot angrier than you are. You got a raw deal, for sure."

She didn't say anything, but her head was cocked as if, for the first time since they had started to talk, she was really listening. Her face still wore its withdrawn look, but Jake was encouraged. Deep within her there had to be a healthy need to talk about her anger. If he could just tap that . . .

"Aren't you going to tell me how grateful I should be that my aunt was willing to take me in?" Katherine asked him.

Bingo. She did know how to zero in on the soft spots. That talent must be imbedded in the Holden genes. "The thought did occur to me."

She turned her shoulder away from him, and he knew he'd lost ground. He scrambled to regain the advantage. "On the other hand, I remember somebody telling me I should be grateful I had such good parents that they had the courage to tell me I couldn't buy my own car. I wasn't much interested in how grateful I should be at that moment. I was just angry with them for not giving me what I wanted." He paused. "Maybe you're a little bit angry at your parents for leaving you."

"That's not true." Her chin shot up, her eyes glistening with tears and the anger she wouldn't—couldn't—admit she felt.

"Good," he said hastily, feeling his way again. He knew that to tell her she was denying the truth would destroy what little rapport he had with her. "It would be natural to feel some anger, though. It's one of the stages of grief."

She looked strangely adult standing there on the edge of the water, her chin up. Not unlike Alex in one of her tougher moments. His heart reacted strangely to the thought.

"I can't...seem to do anything right. I can't even...let myself...remember them. It...hurts too much." She looked down, scuffed a shoe in the sand. "I don't belong anywhere anymore. I don't belong at school and I don't belong with Alex." Her large eyes turned to him again. "Her marriage broke up because of me."

Clearly, she wanted him to deny it. "It wasn't your fault Alex's marriage didn't work out," he said, his voice husky with sincerity. "Trust me on this one, Katherine. If two people really love each other and want to work things out, they will. I have a feeling the relationship was in trouble long before you came along."

In the soft evening light, Katherine's face grew reflective. She thought of other things and her face lost animation and color, as if the life had been drained from her. She stood staring out to sea as if she were facing a firing squad. "It's my fault my parents died. They were going to Anchorage to look at a school because they thought I needed a better one. If it hadn't been for me, they'd be alive."

Jake's stomach clenched in sympathy. This was where the trouble really lay. Guilt was the heaviest burden of all. How quickly she had taken it up. "That's nonsense and you know it," he said, hoping he sounded convincing. "Your parents died because they got caught in a storm in a small plane. It could happen anywhere, anytime. They were in that storm because they cared about you. They wanted you to have the best." He took a breath. "They still do. They don't want you to be racked with guilt for something you're not responsible for."

Katherine's eyes filled with tears. She shook her head and turned back to the ocean again, her back stiff, her determination to hide her pain heartbreaking. That was exactly the trouble, Jake thought. She was trying to carry the burden of grief and guilt alone. How long would it take to convince her she could share the load?

STANDING AT THE WINDOW, Alexandra watched Jake and Katherine walk away. She watched the kite skitter, rise, fall and then, under the coaxing of Jake's expert hand, lift on the breeze. Katherine didn't even look up. The girl's pale blond hair fell forward around her face as she bent her head, ignoring the kite—and Jake.

But Jake wouldn't be ignored. He stopped, reeled the kite in. Katherine stood beside him, her hands thrust in her jeans pockets as she stared out at the sea. Then she turned. They stood facing each other like two opponents in the ring. The girl's stance told Alexandra that Katherine had gone on the defensive with Jake, just as she did with everyone else.

Alexandra closed her eyes against a stab of pain. It had been too much to ask Jake to accomplish in twenty minutes what she hadn't been able to do in two years. Still, she had hoped he could help. Jake had an incredible knack of seeing into another person's mind.

He looked like he hadn't succeeded in breaching the walls Katherine had built up.

Alexandra moved away from the window. If she knew Jake, and she did, he wouldn't give up. He would keep trying to reach Katherine. And so would she. Maybe together they could do what she hadn't been able to do alone.

ON THE NIGHT of the gallery opening, Alexandra stepped from her car into the hot, wet scent of a Florida evening, feeling as if the insects were chittering a scolding meant for her.

She was an hour late. She'd waited too long for a promised call from Jenkins about the mall property before she'd finally called him, only to be told that he'd left for the day. If that wasn't enough frustration, she'd put her thumb through her hose while she was dressing. Rather than change her stockings, she'd improvised a different outfit than the dress she'd planned to wear. She pulled on black, silky harem pants, topping them with a draped, white satin blouse. Her anxiety mounted as she stroked mascara on her pale lashes and fastened her hair with gold combs. Would anyone come to the opening? Had she raised Kurt's hopes for nothing?

She crossed the sidewalk where her footprints lay embedded in the concrete. Half a dozen well-dressed men and women stood outside the door, obviously waiting until the crowd inside cleared so they could go in. Her anxiety fell away and her spirits soared. The project she'd fought for from concept to reality, the project people had warned her was doomed to fail, had succeeded. She maneuvered her way inside, thinking that the size of the crowd would ensure that several Creighton works would wear sold signs by the end of the evening.

Kurt had asked to escort her tonight, but she'd declined. She wanted him to feel free to mingle and meet all those who wanted to talk to the artist.

Inside the gallery, the crowd milled around Kurt where Lealda Dexter-Smythe held court. The recognized dowager queen of Marathon had a black-gloved hand wrapped around Kurt's arm, and was well on the way to monopolizing him. At the other end of the room, Chas Gordon stood pondering Kurt's largest work, which was hanging in a prominent place on the south wall.

The possibility of seeing Kurt's most unconventional work hang in the lobby of First National brought a smile to her lips. She checked the refreshments table and saw that the flowers were still fresh-looking and the punch bowl was full. She began making the rounds, greeting people as she went. She ended up alone in front of an abstract painting with flowing lines and great slashes of red that Kurt had captioned *Temptation*.

"Take the whites of two eggs," murmured a too-familiar masculine voice in her ear, "mix with a half-gallon of Silly Putty. Daub liberally with two bottles of catsup. Serves twelve."

The trouble was, it was a good description. She tried to stifle the smile tugging at her lips. She shouldn't encourage Jake. He was outrageous enough already. She

turned to face him, fighting to keep a sober expression.
"Aren't you out of your element?"

"Aren't you out of yours?"

"Stop being a thorn in my side."

He raised an eyebrow and looked insufferably sure
of himself. "But it's such a lovely side. And I'm such a
good thorn."

This man didn't need encouragement, he needed
locking up. She could see that he liked her black and
white slink. She wished he had spent a little more time
and thought on his clothes. His chocolate-brown hair
was mussed, his beige sports jacket made of some in-
describable material, his jeans well-worn. Yet, in this
crowd of beautiful people, there was an assurance
about him, a feline grace that no tailor could provide
with a suit of clothes. With his lean-hipped body completely under his control, he looked almost predatory.
Every other man in the room suddenly seemed over-
dressed, overcautious, and insipid in comparison.

"Alexandra?"

She turned to find Kurt Creighton coming toward
her, Mrs. Dexter-Smythe in tow. Kurt was six-foot-
three, a gentle giant. He looked utterly helpless—and
desperate to be free of the woman.

Alexandra opened her mouth to introduce Kurt to
Jake, but Lealda snatched the conversational initiative
away. "My dear Alexandra, what a wonderful evening
you've provided for us. We're all so grateful to you for
badgering us—" she paused, then smiled, as if to soften
the implication of the word "—into seeing this project
through."

Alexandra smiled, too. The woman had refused to
part with a cent of her considerable fortune to make a

donation to the gallery building fund, and had spoken out against it at every opportunity. Now that it was a success, she'd conveniently forgotten that she'd led the loyal opposition.

"And this is our new young doctor, dear Helen's son. How nice to see you again, John Hustead."

"Ma'am." Jake bowed his dark head respectfully, his face bland politeness.

"Helen tells me you two are old friends." Lealda's keen eyes glided from her examination of Jake to Alexandra.

"Very old friends," Jake drawled before Alexandra could speak.

Kurt moved closer and put his arm around her. "It's always nice to meet an old friend of Alex's."

"We used to play doctor together," Jake said with a maddeningly unperturbed expression. "She liked looking at my. . . stethoscope."

She was going to kill him. Slowly, without mercy, enjoying every minute of his suffering.

Jake's gaze shifted to Kurt. Deliberately, his eyes played over the blond hair tied in a braid, the corduroy jacket that was more disgraceful than his own, the diamond earring. Alexandra broke the sudden, awkward silence by introducing them, aware of Lealda's bright blue eyes shrewdly examining Jake's face, Kurt's, and hers.

Jake wasn't helping matters, either. He continued to study Kurt with an intensity that bordered on insolence.

Lealda lifted her eyes to Alexandra. "I've asked Doctor Hustead to join the chamber of commerce.

Perhaps in another year or so, he'll feel settled in enough to serve on the zoning board with us, Alexandra."

"How thoughtful of you to give the good doctor such a warm welcome."

"It's no trouble at all," Lealda smiled a Cheshire cat's smile, and the rope of diamonds at her throat gleamed.

Alex took a determined grip on Kurt's arm. "I really must introduce the artist to some people who've just come in. If you'll excuse us . . ."

She nodded at Jake, her lustrous eyes burning with a fire that promised retribution the moment she could get him alone.

In response he bowed his head, showing that the message was received and understood.

Jake watched her move away, her nicely rounded hips swinging under the black silk. She looked good, too damned good, in the white top that folded loosely over the high mounds of her breasts and those black silk pants that drifted sensuously around her thighs. Good enough to *eat*.

He supposed he shouldn't have made that crack about playing doctor. They hadn't done that kind of experimenting, not really. He probably wouldn't have said it if that big ape Creighton hadn't put his arm around Alex's waist. How deeply was she involved with him? He'd have a couple of things to say to her about that.

He hoped she hadn't developed scruples since she'd grown up. He was in the mood for one of those good-old-days, no-holds-barred, down-and-dirty fights. Then a voice inside his head whispered, *Are things any different from when you were sixteen? Did you pick a fight with Alex tonight because you want to take her to bed and can't?*

"Certainly worth watching," murmured Lealda.

Jake was startled from his thoughts by an unpleasant sense of having been caught out.

"Perhaps we can get you on the board sooner, Doctor. I'd enjoy seeing you and Ms. Holden in action—hammering out some of the weightier issues that come before us. I have a feeling it could be the most interesting thing I've seen in years." She smiled and turned to the painting they'd been looking at a moment ago. "Strange-looking thing, isn't it? Do you suppose he used catsup to get that shade of red?" As she drifted away, Jake decided he liked Lealda Dexter-Smythe after all.

AROUND MIDNIGHT, Kurt pulled up in front of Alexandra's house, switched off the engine and turned off the headlights. He sat in the dark staring straight ahead in a way that made Alexandra feel uneasy. The warm, shadowy Florida night was too close, too intimate.

Determined to keep things light, she reached over and patted his hand. "Happy?"

"Yes, thanks to you." He turned in the seat. She could just make out the shadow of his head, the star-gleam of his diamond stud. He clasped her fingers and brought them up to his lips. His mouth felt too full, too pliant against her sensitive fingertips. "I owe it all to you."

He was grateful, that was all, Alexandra told herself. Natural enough under the circumstances. "You don't have to thank me, Kurt," she said lightly. "I wanted to do it for you and for the gallery."

"The gallery can't show its appreciation. I can."

"And you have. Very nicely."

He turned her hand and rubbed his mouth on her palm. "Not nearly as nicely as I'd like to."

She was stunned by his ardor. "But we agreed—"

"No," he said softly. "You proposed an arrangement that excluded sex and I went along with it because I was too busy working on the show to give you my full attention. Did I tell you how beautiful you look tonight?" He toyed with the drape of her blouse, his fingers brushing against her bare neck. Her uneasiness escalated. She moved nervously forward on the seat, her silk pants rustling in a warning whisper.

"No, of course you didn't—"

He leaned over and kissed her shoulder. Alarmed, she said, "Kurt, this isn't like you."

He raised his head and in the dim light, she saw the rueful curve of his mouth. "You don't like it."

She was lost in a maze of conflicting emotions, amazement the dominant one. "This is your night, a triumph, the night we've both been waiting for. Don't let's spoil it by complicating it with sex—"

"Sex doesn't complicate things. It simplifies things."

"Not for me—"

He made an impatient sound and tugged her into his arms, taking her mouth with a determination that told her he was tired of being put off.

When she didn't respond, he let her go, a soft succinct word escaping his lips, a word muttered with a heartfelt emotion she hadn't thought him capable of.

"Kurt, this isn't the way it should be."

"What's the matter? Isn't the world going according to your plan?" He sounded bitter, almost angry. She seemed to have struck a raw nerve in him. "Oh, what the hell. I knew better."

She sat very quietly beside him. "I thought we both did."

He stared out through the windshield. "You thought wrong."

"I'm sorry."

"So am I." He turned his head to stare at her. "So is this Jake the new man on the scene?"

"He isn't a new man, he's an old friend, just like we said. We really did share a playpen—"

"And a jolly spot of playing doctor on the side."

"Don't pay any attention to Jake. We've known each other for a long time. He has a big-brother fixation on me, nothing more." She laid her hand on his arm and said gently, "You had a wonderful success tonight. Please don't spoil it by trying to change things between us."

He sat motionless under the pressure of her hand.

"Perhaps I'd better go. You can take the car home." She opened the car door, hoping he wouldn't say something conciliatory before letting her leave.

"No, I'll walk," he decided.

"But it's almost two miles—"

"I need the exercise." He opened the door on his side and then turned back to her. "I may be busy over the next few days," he said stiffly. "Too busy to call."

She'd hurt his pride. She couldn't blame him for trying to save face. "I understand. Good night, Kurt." He wouldn't look at her. He wasn't going to say "sweet dreams" the way he always did.

She climbed out of the car. He did the same. She could hear the gravel crunch under his feet as he walked away.

AT THE TOP OF THE STAIRS, a small light burned in the living room. Beatrice had left a lamp on for her, a considerate, comforting touch. Then why did it make her feel so alone?

It reminded her that she was destined to live a lifetime of coming home to one lit lamp left by her mother. But why?

On a warm, sweet night like this one, she almost forgot why.

Crazy. She hadn't felt this empty, this needy, in a long time. It must be Kurt's talk of sex that made her think of hot sweet nights and lonely beds.

If she worked hard at it, and closed her eyes to a few truths, she could blame Jake for what had happened. It was an old habit, blaming a failed relationship on Jake. In the early days, when she was still a believer in romance, the boys in her life had suffered by comparison. None of them were as funny, as intelligent, as quick to understand as Jake was. In her later teens, Jake had nipped her romances in the bud just by being there and acting like a protective brother.

She's lost the habit of using him as a convenient whipping boy. What had happened tonight wasn't Jake's or anybody's fault, it was a misunderstanding between Kurt and her. She'd thought Kurt understood—and accepted—her need for a platonic friendship. He'd decided that if he bided his time, she'd change her mind. Jake had gotten accidentally thrown into the coil of her life, and she'd have to extract him from it as soon as possible.

She opened the door. Jake was sitting there waiting for her.

He lounged in Beatrice's knitting chair, his long legs stretched out and crossed at the ankle. His jacket slung over the back of the chair as if he had the right to make himself at home. He sat with his chin tipped forward onto his chest, every muscle relaxed, his hair shiny in the lamplight. He looked mature, masculine. Henry Higgins waiting for a wandering Eliza to come home.

Strange little shocks danced over her nerves. "This is an unexpected . . . pleasure."

He tilted his chin up and looked her over with mock surprise, as if he hadn't expected to see her. "Hello, Alex." His greeting was as cool as hers. He looked half-asleep, but Alexandra knew a quick, sharp alertness lay under that lazy smile.

She dropped her purse on the table, her heart sinking. She felt raw, vulnerable, too fragile after her parting with Kurt. She didn't feel like going one-on-one with Jake. Yet what better time than this to make him understand that he couldn't go on interfering in her life the way he had at the gallery.

"You haven't waited up for me since we were sixteen," she said, resigning herself to the inevitable. Alexandra folded her arms and imitated his detached look. "I like it even less now than I did then."

He stared at her steadily, not an eyelash flickering.

"I'm a grown woman, Jake. I don't need you to—"

"Are you grown-up enough to ask him for a medical report before you start sleeping with him?"

She should have been surprised, but she wasn't. She'd known what was on Jake's mind the moment he'd met Kurt. She matched his gaze, giving him back a taste of his own cool nerve. "How do you know I haven't already slept with him?"

"I could tell by the look in his eyes. He's still hungry. And you're home too early."

"Maybe we're quick."

The expression on his face told her what he thought of that retort. "Answer the question."

Her chin came up, her eyes flashed. "It's none of your business."

"It is if it concerns your health. Or your life. Come off it, Alex, this is Jake you're talking to. You know the dangers as well as I do."

She took a step closer. "What does it take to get through to you? I'm an adult. I've been living quite nicely without your advice for the past several years, and I intend to go on doing so for the next several." Her eyes locked with Jake's. "I'm not part of you."

"Aren't you?"

Those two words—a husky drawl—held a world of intimacy.

"Go home, Jake."

Slowly, lazily, he uncurled his long body and rose to his feet.

She stood very still, watching him as he took the first step toward her, and the second, and the third.

In a split second he'd changed from old friend to combatant in the oldest game of all. He'd become a member of the opposite sex. Whose mind you couldn't read. Each of her senses was alert.

"Don't . . . do this."

"Do what?" He reached out and touched a silken strand of hair that lay on her neck, his brilliant green eyes playing over her face. "Did he kiss you?"

She raised her square chin up another notch. "Yes."

"You didn't look kissed when you came in. You weren't wearing a lovely flush under your skin like you are now. He didn't even scrape the surface, did he? You've been letting me go on at you when there's nothing at all between you and Kurt. Why, Alex? What are you so afraid of?"

He was close enough to touch and she found herself touching him, her palms on his cotton-covered chest. She felt locked with him inside a golden circle. "Let me go," she said. He'd mesmerized her with those green eyes, drawn her close and captured her.

"I'm not touching you," he said softly. "You're the one who's touching me."

She moved to snatch her hands away, but he caught her wrists and pressed her hands against him. "Dammit, no, Alex. Leave them there." He looked dark, intent, determined to make her acknowledge the truth. "For once in your life, admit that you enjoy touching me as much as I like having you do it."

His words and the heat of his body under her hands made sexual desire rise in her, burning, heated, too strong to be denied. "You've got to let me go." Her mouth was stinging, aching to be kissed.

"You want me to kiss you, I know you do. Say it, Alex."

She shook her head. Her skin burned and her body ached, but she couldn't give in to the yearning need, to the desire to have a glimpse of paradise. It was a cruel sham, that paradise. It held regrets and sorrow and recriminations. She lifted her head and met his eyes with hers. "I want you to let me go."

A fire flared in his eyes. If she didn't know him so well, she might have been afraid. Then, he released her and stepped back. "As you wish." His words mocked her.

"It's very late. Perhaps you should leave." She felt oddly ashamed, as if she had done him a great wrong.

Jake smiled that deep, ironic smile that said everything and nothing, turned to pick up his jacket, his face shielded from her by the breadth of his shoulders. Was it the sound of his breathing she heard, or her own?

Lazily, he turned around, dangling his jacket over his shoulder. He looked composed, but the darkness in his eyes told her his composure was costing him. "I'd like a rematch. Care to meet me in a foggy grove at dawn?"

She shook her head, grateful that he was trying to lighten the mood, but unable to respond in kind. "I don't want to fight with you—" her face smooth and clear, her body slowly coming back under control, she added softly "—or make love with you."

"You're a coward, Holden."

"I know who I am, Jake. Better than you do."

"Do you?" His hand on the knob, he turned to face her. He wore a wise, knowing look she recognized. "I wonder."

He left the room, then she heard the screen door slam behind him—a hollow, lonely sound echoing into the hot night.

3

SHE STOOD IN THE BATHROOM, a paste bucket in one hand, the brush in the other, the new wallpaper in a roll at her feet. Her mind wasn't on her work. She resented feeling the way she felt—alive, restless, full of hope. Insidious, soul-destroying hope. Wasn't she too old—too smart—too hope? She knew who she was, what she wanted. Jake wasn't going to change that.

She wouldn't let him. She wanted to stay exactly like she was. Safe.

Then you'd jolly well better keep your hands off him.

That was the thing that bothered her the most. Why was it that Jake had only to come within touching distance and she touched? He had grabbed her wrists, but not until she'd reached out to him. It was as if he had a power over her that she couldn't resist.

Alexandra lifted the paste brush and applied a glistening coat to the bathroom wall, her mouth tight. The man was intruding on every part of her life. He was even the reason she was wallpapering today.

He'd done his mother's bathroom last weekend in a powder-blue paper with little daisies. He must have enjoyed every minute of it, knowing how competitive their mothers were, knowing Helen would show off her newly covered walls to Beatrice and Beatrice would go to Marathon the next day for her new wallpaper. And that was exactly what she'd done. When she came home, she'd turned soulful eyes on Alexandra and said that she shouldn't have bought the paper—that Alexandra was so busy at the office and she did so much for them already, she mustn't even think she wanted her to do it—although the bathroom had been drab for the longest time and she was so anxious to have it done before her birthday next week. Well, never mind. They would just have to wait for the paperhanger, even though he couldn't come for three months. . . .

The wallpaper flowers were pink and yellow, pretty enough, but they had a diabolical matching pattern that was giving her fits, especially when her concentration wasn't what it should be.

She climbed on the step stool and held the edge of the paper up against the ceiling edge, flattening it with her one clean palm. It was a tiny bit crooked. It didn't quite fit. She never could get that first piece to fit.

She couldn't get love to fit, either. To hope, to dream, to think of love everlasting was something she hadn't done in a long time. Since her breakup with Clay, she'd broken herself of the silly habit of wishing on a star.

Love wasn't everlasting. Life got in the way, careers got in the way—people got in the way.

People didn't know how to love. And she knew how least of all.

Because she couldn't love just *a little*.

That's what the men in her life had wanted her to do. Love them just a little. Not enough to interfere with their life-styles, but enough to be there when they needed her.

You expect too damned much. These had been her father's words when she'd confronted him after he'd finally come home from a business trip in Europe. While he was wheeling and dealing, her mother had lost their third and last child. Beatrice had cried out for her husband, needing him. Alexandra had been thirteen, with an adolescent's fierce sense of justice and loyalty. She'd put in the overseas call to her father. Adam Holden had told her he couldn't come home, not just then. Alexandra had hung up the phone, her face white, her teeth clenched. It had been up to her to comfort her confused and frightened eleven-year-old brother. And when her mother had come home from the hospital and lay grieving and inconsolable in her bed, Alexandra had ferried juice, medication, pillows and gelatin to her, urging her to take care of herself. When her mother had refused, Alexandra had shamelessly used her father's return home as the carrot on the stick, telling Beatrice that Adam wouldn't want to see his beloved wife looking so weak and wan. The ploy had worked. Beatrice had begun to eat and take an interest in life again.

One part of the young Alexandra's mind had marveled at the lie that had rolled off her tongue so glibly, but the practical side of her had whispered that it had been necessary. In the week since her mother had awakened in the middle of the night with labor pains, she'd matured enough to know what things had to be done for her family, and she'd realized that she was the one to do them.

When her father came home at last, he was greeted with loving kisses from his wife and son. Alexandra stood back, detached. When they were alone, she told him that she thought he'd failed his wife and son miserably.

Instead of hearing her words for what they were, a cry of pain and a need to shift the responsibility of the care of her family to more adult shoulders, he lashed back at her, telling her she was an overbearing, spoiled young lady who took advantage of everyone around her, including her mother. What did she know about success and failure? Who did she think worked for this family, made the money it needed? Just exactly who did she think paid for the designer jeans she wore, the fine house she lived in, the food she ate? She needed to be taken in hand. And he would see to it, as soon as he got home from Colorado. Unfortunately he was leaving in the morning but when he returned, he would deal with her.

By the time he came back, he'd forgotten all about their argument and his threat. She might have respected him more if he'd cared enough to punish her.

It had taken her a long time to forgive her father and let herself fall in love. When she did, she foolishly picked a man just like him. Clay was dedicated, totally committed to his political career. Ironically, that was what had drawn her to him. She had admired his single-minded dedication. She had loved him for what he was and what he intended to become. She thought they would have an ideal life working together toward the same goals.

But when her brother and his wife were killed, and she'd told Clay she wanted to take Katherine into their home, she'd discovered their goals weren't alike at all. Clay hadn't wanted the burden of raising another man's child. He hadn't wanted her to assume the responsibility, either. He wanted all Alexandra's love and attention. They argued about it incessantly...until one rainy day she discovered Clay didn't want any child to clutter up their lives, not Katherine, not even one of their own.

She wouldn't make the same mistake again. She wouldn't get involved with a dedicated man, no matter how well she knew him or how much she liked him. Jake was as wrong for her as Clay had been, as Kurt had been. She admired and respected dedication. She just couldn't live with it.

She pulled the paper off and refit it to the wall, stretching up to align the edge with the ceiling. Sweeping over the paper with long strokes, smoothing the wrinkles rhythmically as she went, she climbed off the step stool and heard a sound behind her.

Jake stood leaning against the doorway, his mouth twisted in a smile that was mocking but sympathetic, his brown hair wearing its perennially mussy look. He wore a pair of white shorts and nothing else. They were crisp white cotton ones that stood out from his thighs, not in the least suggestive. But they were short enough to make his muscular legs look even longer.

"Having fun?"

The question was casual, light. If that's the way he wanted to play it, she'd go along. "Loads. I'd like to thank you—and my mother—for making this afternoon possible."

Jake smiled, but his eyes were oddly untouched by his amusement. "Mom is talking about ripping out the patio and putting in flagstone next weekend."

Alexandra groaned in genuine horror. "Can't you talk her out of it?"

Jake met Alexandra's gaze steadily. "You could tell your mother she can't have everything Helen has."

"Now why didn't I think of that?"

"Because you're too intent on giving her everything she wants, to make up for what she lost...just like you do with Katherine."

And she thought he didn't know her as well as he once had. She was as transparent as glass to him. "I'm not trying to make it up to Mom for Dad's death."

"No? Okay, if you say so. But if you weren't trying so hard to be everything to everybody, you wouldn't be looking so tired right now. And you'd let me help you do that." He nodded at the roll of wallpaper, the water tray, the paste she'd mixed.

"No, thanks. There's not enough room for two people to work in here."

He leaned against the doorway looking monumentally unmoved by her rejection. "I'll just keep you company then."

Exasperated, she glared at him. "Jake, please. I need all my concentration to do this."

He gave her a bland, innocent look and folded his arms across his broad, bare chest. "How could I possibly interfere with your concentration, just standing here?"

Let me count the ways.

She turned away from him and began to work, more from a need to put him out of her sight than an interest in getting the job done. She measured a length of wallpaper and climbed on the ladder with the wet paper dangling over her shoulder. She pressed the paper onto the wall quickly, her heart not in her work. Was he ever going to stop watching her?

She released the top of the paper and moved her hands down to smooth out the lower portion. The wallpaper rolled off the wall and landed on her head.

She managed to untangle herself from the wet pasty paper and shoot a warning look at Jake. "If you laugh, you're dead."

"Me, laugh? Why would I do that? I don't see anything funny happening here." But the muscles at the side of his mouth and jaw were twitching. Smooth as silk, he added, "Sure you don't want any help?"

She came down off the ladder and headed straight for him, pasty fingers spread out, the devil in her eyes—she looked like a sickly Frankenstein intent on murder. Disgustingly sure of himself, he didn't move a muscle—until her hands were an inch from his face. He caught her sticky wrists and green eyes clashed with silver-blue. "Admit you need help," he said, "and I'm yours."

Eye to eye, toe to toe, chest to chest, it was impossible to lie to him. "I . . . need . . . help."

He relaxed visibly, his grip on her wrists loosening, the control on his mouth loosening, too. His smile was easy, friendly and contagious. "Now that wasn't so hard, was it?"

Softening her up was too easy for Jake. He created not only a chink in her armor but also a neck-to-toe rent, and he'd made it look like child's play. She'd never been very good at asking for help. She'd wanted to be independent, had been independent from the time she was thirteen and learned how little she could depend on her father.

As if he'd been doing it for years, Jake brushed past her, plucked the coiling strip of paper off the lid of the toilet and carried it up the ladder with him. He pressed it against the wall, and of course, the traitorous paper stuck instantly.

Jake was good at making things stick, both wallpaper and lessons.

He made it seem natural for them to work as a team. He climbed the step ladder and fit the next piece to the ceiling edge, while she took the scissors and did the close-fit cutting at the bottom. It seemed easy to laugh when he came down the ladder with paste on his nose. And easy to have him tease her about being a poor executive if she hadn't had the sense to delegate a job like this. It was easier still to tease him about being the real fool, since he'd volunteered to help.

Three hours later, she sat cross-legged on the floor beside him, laughing, swiping his arm with paste and getting swiped in return. She threatened him with her sticky hands, reaching for his hair. He caught her wrist, his eyes a high-sea green.

"Hey, bright eyes, call off the hostilities. We're done in here."

"Oh, are we?" She'd been so intent on bedeviling him, she'd hardly noticed.

"I think I'll go home and get cleaned up. That is, if I can get out of here without sticking to the wall." He did a cross-eyed scarecrow, Cary Grant style, too darn good-looking to be really scarey.

She laughed because it was a relief to be with him and not feel that sexual tension, that physical tug of need. How silly they must look, sitting on the floor of the bathroom, threatening each other with sticky hands like playschool children. And how silly she was to worry about things changing between them. They had always been friends and they always would be. They were never meant to be lovers.

Then his knee touched hers. And his eyes met hers. As quickly as that, desire flared deep and low within her.

He knew. "I'd help you up," he said, "but I'm afraid you'd be stuck to me for life."

His words were spoken too casually to have the obvious double meaning. She strove to behave as casually as he. "And we couldn't have that, could we?" She used the edge of the tub to lever herself upright. He followed suit. She had bare feet so he seemed much taller than she.

"I owe you one, Hustead."

Something flickered in his eyes—amusement, audacity. "I'll remember that." He pivoted to the sink and turned the water on over his hands, rubbing them with a bar of soap.

"Towels are underneath." She didn't want to stand there watching him in the intimacy of the bathroom, seeing the muscles in his back move as he scrubbed his hands. He had a nice back, long, lean and muscled, the kind of back that invites tantalizing strokes. Alexandra swallowed and retreated behind a mask of politeness. "It was nice of you to come over and help me."

He reached for a towel, extracted a blue one from the cabinet and snapped it out while he turned to her. He wiped his hands carefully and said, "I'm a helluva nice guy."

"I know that." Their eyes met, then hers dropped.

"Your turn." He gestured at the sink.

She hesitated and then stepped forward. He turned on the water for her, his eyes never leaving her face. She concentrated on scrubbing the paste off her hands, but she could feel him watching her intently. When he handed her the towel, she took a breath and said what she'd been wanting to say. "I do want to be your friend, Jake."

"Thanks." The word had a tiny bite in it, but his face was bland. "Well, I guess I'll be going home. The ladies should be finished with their tea and crumpets." He turned his back on her and strolled out of the bathroom.

That's it? He was leaving her without saying a thing, without acknowledging her attempt to make amends? She ran out of the bathroom and down the hall into the living room in time to see the white corner of his shorts going out the door. "Jake!"

He stopped, turned, his expression politely curious.

"Pizza tonight?" she asked. "I'll buy this time. It's the least I can do after all the time you spent helping me this afternoon."

He hesitated and she had the distinct impression he was going to say no. She wanted him to say yes, needed him to say yes. "Ask Helen to come, too."

The tension drained away from his face, leaving a composure that made him look like a stranger. "Sure, if that's what you want."

"Six o'clock," she told him.

"Six o'clock it is." With the grace of a timber wolf, he ambled through the door and down the steps.

THAT NIGHT Jake gritted his teeth and made a massive effort to control his body. He wasn't sixteen any more. But he hadn't quite got the knack of acting cool, wary and withdrawn when his body burned with desire. Which happened when he was around Alexandra.

It was hard to act cool and wary over pizza. Pizza tended to keep a man humble. A little tomato sauce on the nose, a little cheese on the chin made a commoner out of a king any day.

He didn't mind looking humble—or human. He did mind trying to hide the effect Alexandra had on him. She had showered and changed since that afternoon and she wore an outfit—shorts and tank top—that displayed lots of bare skin at her midriff and throat. She was sprawled on the floor beside Katherine, a long length of thigh stretched out in front of her that looked tasty as hell. She had the smooth, deep tan of a year-round Floridian and her brown hair was sun-kissed.

He knew what he'd like to kiss. The length of her collarbone. The top of her knee. The tip of her nose. The smile she flashed at Katherine. The sweet lift of her breast.

He put up with the torment as long as he could—eating, drinking, chatting with Katherine, acting casual, trying not to talk to Alex too much—or look at her too much.

His ability to dissemble was fading fast. Alex finished her pizza, put her plate on the floor and flashed one of those thousand-kilowatt, impersonal smiles at him. Her executive smile?

He'd had all he could take. He made some offhand comment about having work to do and maybe he'd better be going. He followed his words with action, unwinding himself from the couch and standing up. Four pairs of female eyes flashed up at him. The two older women and Katherine looked disappointed. The one pair of eyes he cared about most looked politely interested and nothing more.

Once during the afternoon, when they were mixing it up with wallpaper paste and snappy one-liners, he glimpsed a vulnerability in Alex's face that was as far from the light, bright facade she'd put on for him as the sun from the moon. Foolish, how one glance, one look in a woman's eyes could give a man hope. But then, she'd smiled at him and joked as she always did, and he decided it must have been his imagination. She meant what she said. She didn't want him for a lover. Why, he didn't know. What difference did it make? The lady simply wasn't interested.

Now all he had to do was figure out how he was going to go on participating in these friendly little Sunday night affairs ad infinitum without going quietly crazy.

One approach to saving his sanity was to make the evenings as short as possible. He said goodbye to the other ladies, looked down at Alexandra, managed a reasonable smile and inclined his head slightly toward her. When he went to the door, she didn't follow him out.

Outside the Florida air was warm, heavy, alive with the sound of insects. The purple, soft late-evening air enclosed him, the breeze provocative, as light as the touch of Alex's hands. His tired brain rebelled at his tight control and strayed into forbidden territory, to thoughts of Alex, lovely, long-legged, smiling under the lamplight.

He was a fool. Now that he was out of the house and safe, his perverse mind was telling him to march back in there, take hold of her arm and drag her with him out into the moonlight.

He forced his feet to keep to the path that led to his mother's house. On the patio, he slumped down in a chair and stared out at the ocean.

An hour later when his mother came home, he was still sitting there.

Even in the dark, he could feel her concern. Helen was sixty, but she looked years younger. The moonlight silvered her salt-and-pepper hair, her unlined face, her well-kept body. "Is this the work you had to do so urgently?"

He didn't answer her. He half suspected she knew what was bothering him. He hadn't been able to hide anything from her since he was two.

"Would you like a drink?"

"No, thanks." Alcohol was not what he needed. The ocean gleamed under the moon. The night was dark, rich with delights for the senses, a soft breeze lifting the tiny hairs on his arm, a palm tree rustling. It was all too romantic—and totally wasted on him.

"On a night like this, you shouldn't be sitting out here alone."

He closed his eyes. Helen's soft voice was the extra needle he didn't need, reminding him of where he'd like to be and what he'd like to be doing. "Why not? I like my own company."

Helen made a ladylike sound that was as close to a snort as she'd allow herself. "Are you going to do something about Alex or shall I?"

He sat up and tried to see her face, but it was too dark. "Whatever scheme you've got in your pretty little head, forget it."

"You've liked her for a long time."

"I've tolerated her for a long time."

"She's a lovely girl."

"*Woman*, mother, she's a woman."

"I know that. The question is, do you know it?"

His mouth quirked in a half smile. "Oh, I know it. Believe me, I know it." He said it with a little too much emphasis, but then what the hell—he wasn't telling her anything she didn't already know. His mother was a master at creating a restful environment, which was one of the reasons he'd moved in temporarily with her, but she was also a master at destroying it. She could burrow to the heart of a matter quicker than any TV private detective he'd ever seen.

"You know, son, I've always found it hard to admit to a mistake. We try so hard. That's what's wrong, you know, trying so hard. First, we're children, then we grow up, have children, raise them and do what we believe are the right things. When we get a little older, we see we were terribly shortsighted and wrong."

Jake shifted in his chair, feeling uncomfortable. He cast a lazy-eyed look at his mother. "You don't have anything to feel guilty about."

"Don't I?" she wondered with a sigh, her head lifting to look up at the stars.

Jake hitched at his pants and made a restless motion as if he were going to stand up.

"No, don't go. Please listen to what I have to say." His mother gazed out over the ocean as if seeking strength from the star-glow lingering on the water. "I'm sorry I discouraged a relationship between you and Alex all those years ago."

"I don't remember that you did."

"Oh, I did. You were very infatuated with her once, but you were so young. I was afraid you might do something we'd all regret. Young men can be very persuasive...and very cruel after they've gotten what they want." She turned her head to look at him. Her face was a dark shadow. "You're not so young anymore."

He bowed his head, his lips twisting in a smile. "Thank you."

"I didn't mean you were old. I just meant that you're not sixteen now, and neither is Alex."

He said nothing. Did she mean to warn him off again?

She made an impatient sound. "Both of you sitting there pretending nothing's changed and so aware of each other you can hardly breathe. Do you think you fooled anyone tonight with your elaborate politeness?"

"Evidently not," Jake said dryly.

"It was so good of her to make a home for Katherine. Alex is such a good girl—" Jake made a sound in his throat, and his mother amended hastily, "I mean, woman. And she does have such a lovely figure."

Jake clenched his hands around the arm of the lounge chair. "Alex is lovely, she's nice, she has all the sterling qualities a woman should have."

Helen smiled as if his dry, slightly annoyed form of agreement pleased her. "You see? You do still like her. It's never too late, you know. Now that she's free...and so are you—you might find it quite comfortable to—"

"Sweetheart, I hate to burst your bubble, but as a matchmaker, you're a miserable failure. What makes you think I want a woman to be comfortable with?"

"Well, you certainly want to be comfortable when you're in bed with her, don't you?" Helen Hustead asked tartly. "Don't they call that a slow, comfortable—"

Jake made a choking sound and lunged to his feet. The lounge chair buckled under his violent upsurge and collapsed in a clattering heap.

"My dear boy. You *are* a doctor, after all."

She sounded amused. Dandy. With elaborate care and a stiff back, he righted the chair and replaced it to its former position. He turned to her, glad that the darkness made it difficult for him to see her face, or her to see his. "I must have been absent the day they gave the lecture on how to discuss current sexual idioms with your mother and keep your cool."

"Well, I do know a little about such things. How do you suppose you got here?"

He loved her and admired her honesty. He always had. But after several hours of exposure to Alexandra, he felt weakened. "I assume it happened in the usual way. Now, if you'll excuse me, I think I'll go for a run."

So polite, so correct, so discreetly signaling that he'd had enough of this conversation.

"You go right ahead."

As her son strode off the patio and hit the beach running, Helen's eyes were bright in the soft light. "He didn't even stop to stretch his muscles out first. Strange, a good athlete like my son forgetting to do that." She settled back, folded her arms and smiled into the darkness, looking extremely pleased with herself.

A FEW DAYS LATER, Jake Hustead was finishing up a long day's work. He felt as though he'd looked at all the red ears and runny noses of everyone in town under the age of twelve, and he was ready to go home. "Didn't anybody tell these kids they aren't supposed to get sick down here in the sunshine," he grumbled to Janet McPherson, his nurse.

"That's propaganda we natives generate to increase the tourist trade."

"You're no help."

"Is that so?" she replied. Jane was forty, a jewel he'd snatched up out of the list of candidates who'd applied for the job. She'd proved to be as efficient, as down-to-earth and as calm as he'd thought she'd be. She said, "A man came in a little while ago. He said he's a friend. Bob Hastings?"

"Bob Hastings—yeah, I remember him. We were in med school together until he dropped out. What's he doing down here?"

"He has his daughter with him. He wants you to see her."

"What's wrong with her?"

Janet arched an eyebrow. "He wouldn't say. He said he wanted to talk to you. He says it's personal."

"How old is she?"

"Twelve."

Not pregnancy then. At least he hoped not. Jake was bone tired, but he'd grown used to the habit of steeling himself to see just one more patient. He raked a hand through his hair and said, "Give me a few minutes to scrub up, and then show them in to my office. Start a chart on her and leave it on my desk."

Bob Hastings was older, grayer, and a little fuller through the waistline than the twenty-two-year-old man Jake remembered. He was also more nervous. He reached forward to shake Jake's hand eagerly and then stood looking around. "Nice place you've got here."

His daughter had her father's blond hair and green eyes, but her face was delicate and feminine. She was slim and tall, probably close to her full adult height.

Jake told the man it was good to see him, asked what he was doing now and listened while Hastings told him about the sporting goods store he managed in Chicago. Jake invited both of them to sit down. The girl slipped into the chair next to her father's, looking a little like she'd just climbed into a dentist chair.

Jake smiled at the girl and sat back, waiting for somebody to tell him why they were there. Hasting's ruddy cheeks got even redder. "This is my daughter, Melinda."

"It's nice to see you, Melinda."

The girl nodded and looked extremely uncomfortable.

"What brings you to see me today?" Jake asked her.

"My father." For the first time, the girl's eyes met Jake's. He recognized her desperate longing to be somewhere else.

Jake's stomach tightened. Not this child. Please. Not this child.

Jake's green eyes flickered up to Bob Hasting's face. "What is it you want me to do for Melinda?"

"Well, you see I'm separated from my wife and I have custody of Melinda during her school vacations. We flew down here to spend a few days by the ocean, and yesterday Melinda reached a certain point in her development..." he swallowed and struggled on, "and when I found out you were practicing down here, I thought maybe you could...talk to her about it."

"I didn't need to come here," the girl broke in. "I know what's happening to my body. They told us all about it in sex ed."

"I didn't bring you here to hear clinical facts," her father said, patting her arm awkwardly. "I brought you because I want you to talk with somebody about your feelings," he hesitated, "since you won't talk to me."

"I don't want to talk about my feelings. I don't have any feelings to talk about. Besides," she slanted a derisive nod at Jake, "what can *he* know about anything?"

Jake relaxed back in his chair, the tension in the pit of his stomach unclenching. He'd much rather talk to a girl about PMS than tell her she was pregnant. "She's right," he said to Bob. "What do I know about anything?"

"Will you talk to her?" In spite of the cool air in Jake's office, beads of perspiration showed on Hasting's forehead.

"Do you want to talk, Melinda?" He flashed a smile at her. "We can chat for a minute or two, just long enough to get your dad off your back."

Her eyes met Jake's. His were cool and candid, hers defiant. She lifted her shoulders, her indifferent shrug his answer.

With the air of a man being given a reprieve from a death sentence, Hastings stood up. "I'll wait for you in the other room."

Melinda nodded and shot him a look women have given men for centuries when they do something that disappoints.

This was not going to be as easy as he'd thought. Jake unfolded himself from his chair and walked to the small refrigerator he kept in the office for his personal use. Opening the door, he said, "We might as well have something cool to drink while we're going through this little exercise. What's your pleasure, lady, cola, orange, lemon-lime, iced tea?"

"I'll take the iced tea."

"Iced tea it is." He pulled the chilled glasses off the shelf, filled them both and handed one to her. Casually, he propped his rear end on the corner of his desk, his knees close to the chair Bob had vacated so eagerly. He asked her how long she'd been in Florida. She told him three days. He asked her if she liked to swim. She said yes. He asked her where she was staying. She told him the name of a small motel that was located on the ocean side, not far from his mother's house.

She sipped her tea gratefully, as if her throat was dry.

"Do you like being with your dad?" Jake asked casually.

"Yes. Except when he's trying to be the perfect father."

"Is that what he's doing?"

She was trying valiantly to be grown-up and candid, match his casualness and follow his lead into polite adult conversation, but her eyes kept skittering away from his. "He thinks Mom doesn't spend enough time talking to me about . . . things."

"What things?"

With intense concentration, she let her finger trail across the condensation on the outside of her glass. "About . . . being a woman. About being glad I'm a woman. He says Mom never was, so how can she teach me to be?"

"What else does your dad say?"

"He doesn't like to hear me use slang terms like 'the curse' and stuff like that. He says it isn't a curse, and I shouldn't think of it that way."

Jake's opinion of Bob Hasting's ability to nurture a daughter soared. "He's right, you know."

"I know. It's just that, well, it's easy for him to say. The same way it is for you. What do you really know about how it feels?"

"You're right, I don't know how it feels. I only know those same clinical facts you learned in sex ed."

She lifted her head and met his steady gaze straight on, obviously surprised by his honesty. "So aren't you going to tell me how wonderful it is to be a woman?"

"I can't very well do that, not being a woman. From a man's point of view, I think it's pretty wonderful. Someday, you'll grow up and meet a man and he'll think your being a woman is the most wonderful thing in the world. And if you're lucky and the two of you have children, you'll be creating a link to the future for him and yourself." He set his glass of tea on the desk and went over to the wall where his framed diploma hung. There was another framed document hanging next to it.

"See this? It's my family tree." Knowing his audience, Jake said, "Come on. I'll show you where the horse thief is." Jake began at the top of the tree. "These are the two people who started it all, Jeremiah and Annie Hustead. Jeremiah was a paymaster in the Pennsylvania Rifle Regiment under the command of Sam Miles. He administered the oath of allegiance to the people of Washington County, Pennsylvania, in 1777. His son Michael was a fifer in the 8th Pennsylvania Regiment. Michael married a titled lady from England, Lady Jeruthea Clark. And down here," Jake pointed his finger to a branch of the tree, "is his son, Frederick Hustead. They found this on his tombstone in Cameron, West Virginia. Can you read it?"

Melinda moved closer. "Died in 1832. Hung for stealing a horse. May God have mercy on his soul."

"He was a doctor, too. I tell myself he did it because he needed transportation to deliver a baby. But he may have just wanted the horse."

"This is neat. I wish I had a horse thief in my family tree."

"If you look long enough," Jake said dryly, "you'll probably find one. Don't tell your father I said that."

"I won't." Melinda flashed a smile at Jake, giving him a glimpse of the woman she would be one day. Suddenly he wanted to say, *Be careful—it isn't as simple as I've made it seem.*

"This one sure has a lot of branches."

"Lady Jeruthea had fourteen children."

"No way, Hosea. If I have kids, it'll be two, tops."

Jake laughed. "Bigger families were needed back then to populate the country and work the farms. Children added to the economic wealth of families by providing another pair of hands. Then too, not every child lived to reach adulthood. Many died in infancy or of childhood diseases."

Melinda's finger followed another four branches of the tree down to the bottom. "This is you down here?"

"That's me. Look back up here, Melinda." He caught her finger and brought it back to his great-great-grandfather. "If this man hadn't married a second time, I wouldn't be here today."

"No kidding?"

"No kidding. He had nine children by his first wife, but when she died, he married again and had one son. That son is my ancestor."

"That's awesome."

He released her hand and stood back. "See what power you women have? The power to change the world."

"That's even more awesome."

"Indeed it is."

Melinda sat in the chair, her brows drawn together in a thoughtful frown. Had he made any impression? He didn't know. He would probably never know. He'd taken the approach he thought was best, show and not tell. There was so much he'd left out, so much she'd have to cope with on her own. More than he could tell her in twenty minutes. More than she was able to safely absorb right now.

At last she said, "I wonder how I can find out about the people in my family tree."

"Go to a library. They'll tell you how to get started. Your dad can help you." Jake smiled. Bob would love him for volunteering him. What the hell, the guy owed him one, anyway.

4

LONELY. That's the way the house felt when Alexandra walked in after a long day at work. A pencil lay tossed on the kitchen counter—the only sign that her mother had been there.

She didn't want to be alone, not this evening. She wanted company. Company to blot out the empty, aching feeling, to take her mind off the miserable day she'd had. For the first time in a very long time, she hadn't been able to make a prompt, purposeful decision. She hadn't outlined a course of action for Jake's office property or the Hawaiian hotel merger. Now she'd come home to an empty house that emphasized her loneliness—as well as the note on the refrigerator.

Took Katherine shopping. Casserole in frig. Love, Mom.

Out of a long-established habit of efficient paper handling, Alexandra pushed the rainbow magnets aside, crumpled the note and disposed of it. Dispiritedly, she opened the refrigerator door. Chicken casserole as advertised, with croutons on top. Her favorite. But not tonight. She was too tired to eat.

After a shower, she changed into shorts and a halter top and wandered out onto the patio. The cool air helped to partially lift her spirits. But she was haunted by her empty feeling, as if somewhere out there in the hot night was something she wanted and couldn't have.

The telephone rang—a shrill sound that carried through the glass doors of the patio. She rose with a sigh and went inside to answer it.

"Oh, Alex, is that you?" Helen's voice said breathlessly in her ear. "Oh dear, did you just get home? I was hoping—it's about Jake. It's so late and I think he's sleeping in his office again."

Jake had already done that one night last week. His mother hadn't known where he was, and his answering service hadn't been able to raise him on his pager. There had been great fuss and feathers flying until Alexandra had given her key to Helen, who'd driven to the office and found him sleeping in his chair.

"That man needs a keeper."

"I know," Helen said, too quickly. "I'm in the middle of baking a cake. I wonder if you could possibly—"

Baking a cake? Jake's mother was baking a cake at eight o'clock in the evening? That was odd. "It's okay, Helen, really. My car's still in the driveway and I have the key to his house on my ring."

"Thank you, dear. I really do appreciate . . . well, thank you."

The swish of the ocean was the only sound around the Victorian beach house where Jake had his office. The windows were dark and the door was locked, but his car, a black Honda, was still there. He must be walking on the beach. She slipped off her sandals and let them dangle on her finger, as she padded barefoot over the warm sand.

She found him sitting on a bench inside a beach cabana her father had built. The dry rustle of leaves on the roof and the whisper of the surf were the only sounds filling the sultry night as she walked toward him. The moist air was warm on her arms, her legs. He was part of the heat she felt—a long, lean slouch of a man parked on the wooden bench, legs and arms crossed. In the darkness, she couldn't see his eyes. He tilted his head up at her. "What are you doing here?"

It wasn't a friendly opening. But if he thought he was going to put her off that easily, he was wrong. "Your mother sent the cavalry out to rescue you," she said lightly.

"Go tell her I'm alive and well and I haven't drowned or broken my neck."

The dismissal was obvious. She ignored it, clasped a hand around a supporting post and stood in the cabana entrance. "Bad day at Black Rock?"

From the downward tilt of his chin, she knew he'd stopped looking at her and was staring out at the water again.

"Nothing unusual. I managed to make a singular ass of myself, that's all."

A smile on her lips, she came into the cabana and sat down on the bench beside him, her knees angled toward his thighs. She knew the feeling. "So what else is new?"

"I was given an opportunity and I muffed it. A father asked me to explain to his daughter the joys of being a woman. I gave her the biggest bunch of malarkey this side of the Blarney Stone."

"What did you tell her?"

"I told her she had the power to change the world."

"What's so terrible about that?"

He turned to her. "I should have told her the world is tough and smart and she'd better be the same. I should have told her she'd need education and a career and a working knowledge of office politics. Instead, I fed her my family genealogy."

"To show her . . . what?"

"To show her a woman changes the course of history by choosing a certain man to love."

"How long did you have with this girl?"

"Twenty minutes."

"Well, yes, I can see you failed utterly if you couldn't manage to explain the meaning of life in twenty minutes." Alexandra's mouth quirked as she reached down and put her hand over his. The urge to do well, to succeed in every detail of his working day was a characteristic she shared with him. She understood how disheartening it was for him to think he'd failed. "Actually, it sounds as if you improvised rather well. Did you tell her about your horse thief?"

"Of course. He's the best claim to fame I've got. He'll soften up anybody, even the big, tough twelve-year-old women who think they don't need anybody to talk to." He turned to her, as if really registering her presence for the first time. "I don't seem to do too well with twelve-year-olds—you . . . Katherine . . . my patient . . ."

"Don't be so tough on yourself," she said softly. "You're a good doctor. You care about your patients."

He lifted his hand to touch her face. In the darkness, he seemed to be staring at her, trying to see her. "How extraordinary. I didn't know you had the power to soothe."

Her fingers were warm, incredibly warm, hot. The night breeze was cool against her flesh, the ache inside her real. She moved away from his hand. His tension was almost palpable. "What's the matter? Are you afraid of me? I'm harmless."

"You underestimate yourself."

"Alexandra."

Her name was a breath, a whisper. He was going to kiss her and there was no power on earth that could make her stop him. Her need for him was so great that only his mouth could satisfy it.

His lips were cool, firm, and so very right that she trembled with pleasure. His hands came up to grip her upper arms, as if he too felt the need to steady himself.

"Jake, no," she said when he lifted his mouth from hers at last, and they both took a long, slow breath.

"There's nothing to say no to. It's just me." His face was a dark shadow. His hands sought and found her arms. "You're trembling."

He sounded surprised. "It's...been a long time," she told him.

"For me, too." He hugged her closer and flattened his palms on her bare back, more comfort than seduction in his embrace. He seemed cool, calm, unmoved. But she could feel the weight of each of his fingers—she could hear his shallow breathing, feel his body heat. She was caught in a terrible dilemma. He'd told her not to be afraid, which meant the kiss they'd shared was nothing to him. He wasn't really making love to her. So how could she protest? She'd look like a fool if she did, make the kiss seem more important than it was. It was so easy to let him go on holding her. Easy and good.

"I told you about my day," he said softly. "How was yours?"

"Lonely," she said, before she thought. "I needed somebody to talk to and there...wasn't anybody around."

In the silence, the night sang with ocean glitter and starshine. "You can talk to me. I'm a good listener."

He was. Much too good. At that, and at other things. She looked out at the sea. Here in the dark she could say the things she needed to say to him. "I don't know whether to tell this friend of mine that he has to move. If I do, I can sell the property he's occupying and buy a share in a Hawaiian hotel—" she paused "—a little venture with a group of men who aren't sure they want a woman along. A couple of them think including a woman in an investment venture is like taking a female on board ship—bad luck guaranteed."

"They don't know you very well."

"Then there's another property I want very badly, but the owner is a man who is reluctant to sell to a woman. If I could go to him and say I was involved in a Hawaiian hotel merger, he'd sell in a shot. So you see, everything hinges on my being a rotten landlady and kicking my tenant out."

He cupped her chin and smiled down at her. "I had no idea I was the key to so many of your problems. I'll start looking for another place tomorrow."

She put her hand on his. "Thank you. I . . . there's nobody like you, Jake."

"Some people might say that was a blessing."

"Not me."

The night became suddenly still, fired with heat. He leaned toward her, slowly, allowing her time to move away. She stayed where she was, filled with breathless anticipation.

He kissed her carefully—a friend's kiss more than that of a lover.

She pressed gently against his chest. "Jake, I...could get addicted to this . . . this talking and kissing."

"Me, too," he said and smiled. "There's nothing wrong with it. We're just two friends, kissing each other better after a hard day at the office."

"I'd better be going." She looked at him, trying to see his face in the dark. His expression was hidden in the shadow of the ceilinged cabana.

She shouldn't have relaxed. Or trusted him. Without warning, he stood and scooped her off her feet and up into his arms.

"What are you doing? Jake, put me down."

"You need coddling." At the entrance to the cabana, he turned to put her feet through the narrow opening, then carried her out into the star-studded night.

"You idiot." She buried her head against his chest. He smelled warm, clean, familiar. "If anybody sees us, they'll think the worst."

"Or the best." In the reflected light from the surface of the water, she saw his mouth quirk.

The sand gave under his feet as he walked, but she knew he wouldn't drop her. He would keep her safe. Just as he had a moment ago. Just as he always had. She had nothing to fear from him.

By the side of her car, he stopped and let her slide down his body to her feet with the air of a deliveryman depositing his burden in the designated place.

Just as the sea breeze wafted over her bare shoulders, cooling her flesh, and she began to relax, he reached out and idly ran a finger down the strap of her halter top. Nerves sprang to life under her skin. Her eyes flicked up to his face, searching for the truth. Was he touching her as a friend—or as a lover? She wanted to protest, but he was being so casual. She would have moved back, but she was wedged between him and the car door, with no place to retreat. Slowly, deliberately, he played with the strap, making the scrap of fabric rub her breasts, giving her the odd sensation that he was abrading her nipple. From deep within her, desire rose, primitive, demanding, tingles spreading to every part of her yearning body.

"When am I going to see you again?"

She struggled to match his composure. "Beatrice is planning a Sunday barbecue."

"Sounds . . . good."

They were discussing safe, prosaic topics. Soon, she would stop feeling as if she'd been shaken to her shoes, and the world would turn right side up again.

He dipped his head and kissed the sweet, soft curve of her breast. She stood stunned, dazzled by the feathery tickle of his hair and the lightning burst of feeling within her. "Jake," she said, but his name was a sigh of relief, and her hands came up to clasp his back.

He breathed her name against her skin—a husky agreement—and nipped her lightly, making her gasp with the sharp sting of pleasure. He licked the tiny wound and murmured words she couldn't understand, words lost in the softness of the night and the sigh of the ocean. He'd branded her and his primitive possession evoked a corresponding wildness in her. Her hands clasped him tighter and her hips sought his, searching for the fit of his body to hers. He groaned and his mouth moved lower, nudged aside the soft cloth of her top, finding her nipple. He found and possessed her, taking her in with a deep sucking sound, his hands on her back pressing her into sweet surrender.

Pleasure rippled through her, wave upon wave. She lifted her hands to his cheeks, felt the bones of his face, the movement of his muscles as he worshiped her breast, the rasp of his beard against her palm. The intimacy of touching him while he was loving her stunned her. He moaned deeply and lifted his head to take her mouth once again and this time, she knew he meant to be her lover.

The heat of the night swept over her, making her want to lie down with him and let him go on exploring her body with that hot, sensuous mouth.

Dangerous. This was dangerous territory, territory she'd explored before with Clay. It hadn't worked, would never work for her. She broke off the kiss and pushed against Jake, opening her mouth to tell him, but he put a finger on her lips.

"Don't," he said huskily. "You don't need to say it. I know." With a careful, delicate precision, he pulled the cotton cup of her halter back over the nipple that he'd sucked. The rasp of the material against her sensitized skin increased her inner aching. As if he understood, he circled a hand around her neck and pushed her head against his chest, making her rest in his arms as if she were a child who needed comforting. And maybe she was. It was humbling to be read so well, to be known so well.

Her cheek against his chest, she leaned against him, unashamedly drinking in the comfort he offered.

He didn't move a muscle. The silence lengthened by degrees. She took a breath to regain her courage and inhaled the salty, musky scent of him. "I can't . . . hurt you, Jake. Not you."

He pushed her away a little to look into her face, his hands warm on the naked skin of her waist, his green eyes alive with passion as they roved over her face. "I thank you for your concern. But I'm a big boy now. I can look out for myself."

"Then please . . . start now."

"All right." He smiled and his grip loosened. She took a step back from him, the soft sand giving way under her bare feet. "Still friends?" He held out his hand to her, his smile endearing. She relaxed and told herself it was going to be all right. He understood and everything would go back to the way it had been.

She smiled and slipped her hand into his. "Still friends."

"I'm glad." One tug on her hand and she was in his arms. He swooped, taking her mouth with all the expertise of a mature man who knows about women and about loving. The shock was physical, sexual. His tongue searched out the dark caverns of her mouth, teasing, retreating, gently searching for the essence of her. She tried to resist, wanted to resist, but he was so passionate, and she was more needy than she'd ever dreamed she was. She wanted to taste him, wanted to be filled by him.

Subtly, carefully, he thrust and withdrew, his possession male and provocative. *Not friends*, he was saying. *Lovers.* She opened to him in hungry compliance.

When at last he broke away from her in the hot night, she drew in a breath and sought desperately for the courage to deny his possession of her. But he tenderly pressed her against his chest, close enough for her to hear the beat of his heart. Or was it hers, thumping so raggedly that it sounded like thunder in her ears? It could be both their hearts, beating together, the way it seemed they always had been.

"I'm sorry I tricked you," he said huskily.

"You should be." Her voice was as unsteady as her knees.

She was sorry, too. Because he hadn't really tricked her. She'd known the instant she'd put her hand in his that he wasn't giving up as easily as it seemed. She'd known—and hadn't drawn back. She was a complete idiot. All Jake had to do was talk about his problems at the office, and she fell into his arms. His dedication, his caring, his interest in a larger world were like an aphrodisiac to her. She'd dropped into the same old trap again. Would she never learn?

She pushed against him, and he let her go. A safe distance away, she lifted her chin. "Is this how you intend to look out for yourself, launching sneak attacks?"

"War is hell," he said softly, grinning as he reached to open her car door for her.

THERE WERE DARK CIRCLES under her eyes when she dressed for work the next morning. She'd lain in bed most of the night wondering what she would do if Jake went on pursuing her, how she could possibly stop him without precipitating an open, irreparable break between them—and if she really wanted to stop him. She had snippets of dreams, one in which Jake had roller-skated to her door and thrown a hand grenade into a house she'd planned to buy. It had been a fantasy house, huge, glass-walled, facing the ocean. She'd been angry with him for destroying it. He was unscrupulous, deliberately trying to destroy her.

People who live in glass houses . . .

You willingly gave him what he wanted. If he had wanted more, you'd have given him more.

INSIDE THE ELEVATOR of her office building, she searched for the state of mind she usually brought to work, her senses honed, eager to tackle a dozen problems with cool detachment and brisk efficiency. Instead, a breeze-swept beach played in her mind's eye, and under her business suit, her body burned with the memory of Jake's hot mouth on her bare skin.

Sarah looked at her oddly as she came into her office. "Good morning," Alexandra said. "Would you draft a letter to Dr. Hustead saying that in accordance with the agreement we reached last night, we expect him to vacate 33 Ocean Trail in thirty days?"

"Of course," Sarah murmured. Her dark eyes were bright with questions, but she was too savvy an employee to ask them.

"Then give Hennings a call and tell him that I'm cleared for action here and that I want to be included in the preliminary discussions on the Hawaiian hotel merger. After you've done that, call Jenkins and suggest oh so subtly that Ms. Holden has made the decision to be involved in the Hawaiian merger and if he's still interested in having her look at his property—" she paused, raising an eyebrow, and gave Sarah a bland smile. "Something along the line of baiting the hook?"

"I know exactly what you want." Sarah was grinning as she turned to leave the room.

Just as Alexandra was feeling quite pleased with herself and reasonably in control, the phone rang and Lea's soft voice announced that Lealda Dexter-Smythe wished to speak to her. Sighing, she lifted the phone to hear Lealda's imperial greeting, followed by an invitation to lunch.

A hundred plausible excuses trickled through her mind, but she couldn't use any of them. Lealda had been instrumental in opening several of the right doors for Alexandra when she'd first taken over her father's real estate office. Her sense of fairness told her she owed the lady.

They agreed to meet at *The Outrigger*, an informal place at the end of the dock where fishing boats for hire were lashed. *The Outrigger* sounded more elegant than it actually was. The eating place had rough wooden floors and curtain-draped entrances, but the food was excellent and the prices reasonable. Alexandra had barely arrived, when Lealda's heels came tapping along the dock behind her. Alexandra turned to greet her.

As usual, Lealda gave no quarter to informality. She was seventy-years-old and five-foot-two inches tall, if given an eighth of an inch, but she countered her short stature by dressing like a model. She looked as if she'd helicoptered in from Paris to the casual world of boats, fish, and weathered wood. She wore a couturier navy suit, a silk blouse, spectator pumps with the spike heels she loved, and her mouth was painted with red lipstick like a Forties movie queen. Her style and bearing guaranteed attention and service. The waitress was beside them even before they sat down in the red imitation-leather booth.

Alexandra refused a cocktail, but Lealda ordered a Bloody Mary and told the waitress she'd come for the crab leg salad that was on special. Alexandra opted for iced tea, clam chowder and the shark sandwich. From the way Lealda was looking at her, she had a feeling she might need to employ a little assertiveness—or, rather, aggressiveness.

Lealda straightened her back before she went on the attack. "I've talked to Judge Hanson about getting that young doctor on the planning board. He's not opposed. He said, 'it's a good idea if we have a doctor present at the meetings in case you give me a heart attack.'"

"Jake is a pediatrician," Alexandra countered, her tone dry.

"That's all right. Delbert Hanson is getting more childish every day." She smiled, inviting Alexandra to share the joke.

Alexandra wasn't in the mood for jokes. If Jake was on the board, it would be one more place she'd have to see him on a regular basis. Sunday nights were bad enough. Now she'd be thrown into his presence every third Tuesday as well. "Have you talked to Jake? He may not want to give up one of his few precious evenings off, just for the sake of community service—"

"I called him this morning. He said he would be more than willing to serve his community, if we think he's capable of doing the job."

"Oh, he's capable, all right."

Lealda threw her a shrewd look, but was prevented from saying anything by the appearance of the waitress bringing their drinks. When the young woman turned and walked away, Lealda removed the celery stalk from her drink and sipped at it, her eyes carefully staying away from Alexandra's as she said, "So it isn't his competence you object to?"

"What makes you think I object to having Jake on the board?"

"You seem less than enthusiastic about the idea."

"I just wonder if you aren't rushing things a bit. Jake has only been here a few weeks, and you want to hand him one of the most influential positions in the community—"

"A position it took you five years to achieve?" Lealda said shrewdly, a lightly penciled eyebrow lifting.

Alexandra took a firm grip on her tea glass and an even firmer grip on her temper. Lealda was an older, more skilled opponent, with an instinctive feel for timing the thrust. Alexandra admired her, but she had a few skills of her own. "How long it took me has nothing to do with my feelings about Jake's inclusion. He hasn't been here long enough to know whether he'll want to stay. It might be prudent to—"

"I asked him about that. He says he is settled in and has no intention of moving back North."

Alexandra lifted her head and met Lealda's knowing eyes. "You seem to have covered all the bases."

Lealda laughed her husky laugh. "I was born knowing how to make a home run."

"Never mind that you have to pitch a few foul balls here and there?"

The gray, carefully made up eyes met hers. "Have I ever pitched you a foul ball?"

Her sense of honesty made her answer, "No."

"Maybe there is something I haven't taught you, though. How to make room on the team for a new player."

"Perhaps I'll learn by doing," Alexandra murmured.

BACK AT THE OFFICE, Sarah followed Alexandra to her desk with a yellow legal pad of messages. "Mr. Creighton called to say that Chas Gordon did decide to buy his work for the First National lobby. That's the good news. The bad news is we've just had a call from Jenkins. He's had a higher bid for the mall property and he's decided to accept it."

"Who got it?"

Sarah raised an eyebrow and drawled, "Dr. Jake Hustead."

Alexandra put on a bland face to disguise her shock. Jake needed new office space—true, but did he have to snatch the very piece of property she'd wanted, out from under her nose? Maybe the deal wasn't firm yet. She'd have to talk to him that evening.

A storm blew up around four o'clock, and by the time she drove home two hours later, torrents of rain splattered against her windshield. It seemed fitting, like the missing piece in the puzzle. What else could go wrong?

She saw what else when she walked into the house and found her mother, Katherine, and Helen seated on a blanket on the floor picnic-style, munching sandwiches and chips by candlelight in the gray light of the stormy evening, and cheerily telling her the power had gone off. Beatrice's elaborately twined candlestick holder sat ceremonially in the middle of the blanket, casting golden light over their faces.

"You look like you're having a seance," Alexandra observed dryly, when she walked past them to head for her bedroom and change out of her soggy clothes.

Beatrice smiled. "What a wonderful idea."

Too tired to respond and dreading the confrontation she meant to have with Jake, Alexandra escaped into her shadowy bedroom, changed into the first thing that came to hand, a pair of short slacks and a loose blouse.

When she came out again, Beatrice said cheerfully, "We've got pastrami, roast beef, turkey, swiss cheese, or tuna. You can have a rye bun, wheat bread, or a slice of sourdough."

Alexandra wished she could stay, sink down beside Katherine on the blanket and pretend she had nothing more earthshaking to think about than the composition of her sandwich. "I need to talk to Jake. Is he at home, Helen?"

Jake's mother turned toward Alexandra, her face shadowed. "Why, I think so, dear. He didn't mention going out. He talked about taking a shower, but he didn't go in before I left. I'm sure he must have gotten it done before the power went off." She hesitated and then said, "You'd better take a candle with you. He wouldn't be able to find mine."

Alexandra turned away from Jake's mother and collected candle and matches. She walked to the door, fervently hoping that he had finished his shower.

The lawn stretched in front of her black and wet, hiding small puddles that her sandaled feet found as she ran. The wind tossed her hair and tried to snatch the candle and matches out of her hand. Lightning snapped fiercely ahead of her, ripping a dagger of light through the blackness. The thunder followed, reverberating over the water.

By the time she reached the Hustead patio, she was out of breath and soaked. The stairs were wet and sleek and so was the railing she clung to. She was glad to reach the overhang where she had some shelter from the wind and rain.

"Jake!" She rattled the handle on the glass door, praying he would hear her above the racket. The palm trees clattered like maracas. The thunder rumbled and the ocean washed relentlessly. The wind was equally unrelenting, tossing a spatter of stray drops on her already soaked blouse. "Jake, open up."

Why wasn't he coming to let her in? Where was he? Her voice rose in panic. "Jake!"

The lightning flared, revealing him behind the glass. The door snapped open and he stood scowling in the opening, naked except for a white towel wrapped around his waist. She scrambled into the room, carefully avoiding him, the rain gusting in behind her.

"What the devil—I thought you were over at your mother's eating pastrami sandwiches."

He shoved the door closed, shutting out the storm, locking her in with him in the sudden silence.

Rattled, she said exactly what she didn't want to say. "You're too scantily dressed to be coming to the door."

"I was taking a shower when the power went off. I thought I'd wait a bit to see if it would come back on, and I could take my second rinse." He paused, and the lightning cracked again, illuminating his face. "I didn't expect to be receiving visitors in a storm like this."

"I wanted to see you." *But . . . not quite so much of you.* She was nervous, not the way she wanted to be at all. She wanted to be cool, calm, businesslike. Instead, she felt warm, disturbed, and convinced she'd made a major error. "I brought a candle. Helen was sure you wouldn't be able to find one."

"I didn't look. Didn't think I needed one just for myself. But now that you're here—"

She didn't want to know if his eyes were going over her, trying to catch a glimpse of her in the darkness. Aware of her wet clothes clinging to her body, she turned away from him and went through the business of lighting the candle, then discovered she had no place to put it. She turned around to him, holding the lit candle, the light flickering in her face.

"Diogenes, in the flesh," he murmured. "You've been looking a long time for an honest man. I wonder when you'll find him." At the look on her face, he shook his head as if disparaging his own words. "I'll get you something to put that thing in before the hot wax drips onto your hand."

Jake strode into the kitchen and, to his great displeasure, found that his hands were trembling. When he'd made that dumb crack about her search for an honest man, she'd looked bleak and vulnerable, like a waif who'd come in from the storm expecting shelter and finding more trouble. She was a soaked, lonely lady he wanted desperately to take in his arms and love.

Whatever she'd come for, it wasn't what he wanted to give her. Keep away, her eyes said to him. And he, great fool that he was, was doing what she'd asked. But looking at that woman, with her lovely face beaded with rain and her soaked clothes revealing the mounded sweetness of her breasts, was something he'd rather not do while he was wearing nothing but a damn towel.

He returned with a half-empty catsup bottle and a dark closed look on his face. Without meeting her eyes, he took the candle from her hand and propped it in the mouth of the bottle. With great ceremony, he carried it to the table in the dining section by the kitchen. Then, he stood back and folded his arms, his face expressionless.

"Can I get you something to drink . . . beer, cola, wine?"

"No. Yes. I'd like a glass of wine, please. Take the candle with you this time."

"No, I'll leave it here with you."

While Alexandra watched, Jake disappeared into the darkness again, a shadow moving around in a house eerily lit with a flickering flame. He came back, his hands full of glasses and the wine bottle, his chest dark and hairy, the muscles of his arms gleaming in the glow of the candle, the towel a primitive loincloth. There were intriguing shadows under his eyebrows, under his chin, in the circle of his navel. Shadows that begged to be explored. Alexandra felt her teeth clench. This was going to be hard, much harder than she'd imagined.

The bottle clinked against the glasses as he poured out the wine. The thunder cracked, making her start. She was glad he had his back to her and couldn't see how edgy she was. She didn't want to feel locked in the safe darkness with him, while the elements raged outside. She'd come over meaning to be very cool, very businesslike. How could a woman be businesslike with a man who wore nothing but a towel and the golden glow of a candle?

He turned. "What shall we drink to?" he asked, his face bland.

"The return of power from the mainland," she answered with a trifle too much fervor.

His eyelashes flickered down, surprisingly long and dark-shadowed, his face relaxing for the first time since she'd come through the door. He was obviously pleased to discover that his bareness disconcerted her. "To the return of power," he said, and lifted his glass.

Determined to be as civilized as he, she drank. The wine was cool and tart on her tongue, typical of Jake. He was a man who'd always liked a sting in his wine, a sting in his life. He was enjoying this moment very much, she thought, and wished she had a bit of his élan. She turned away from him and wandered to the door to watch the storm, her glass in her hand. Looking out at the flare of lightning in the darkness, she said, "Aren't you curious about why I've come?"

"I knew you'd tell me sooner or later. I was hoping it might be later."

She heard a faint rustle, felt him coming to stand beside her. "What I wanted to say to you seems petty now."

"Thunder and lightning, wind and rain have a way of reducing life to the basics."

She took a tighter grip on her glass as well as her emotions. "I was upset because you'd bought some property I was going to buy."

"It was you who was dealing for it then." Jake sounded thoughtful. He hadn't known. She felt ridiculously relieved.

"I did wonder who I was bidding against," he went on. "Are you still upset?"

"No. I realize you were doing what you thought best after our . . . talk the other night. That property will be ideal for you."

"It would have been ideal for you, too. If I had known . . ."

She shrugged her shoulders, not wanting to talk about property any more. "It's all right, really."

"I didn't want to stand in the way of your . . . success." He said the words in a mocking, relaxed drawl that was half kidding, half serious.

She tilted her chin and kept her eyes set on the darkness beyond the door. She was here and he was receptive. She'd better clear the air on all the issues. "I had lunch with Lealda today. She told me you've agreed to serve on the planning board." She turned to him, then, steeling herself for the sight of his dark, sleek-boned face, his hard, graceful, half-naked body. She had herself under control, but it was a tentative hold. Her tone feathery light, she said, "If you go ahead with that, we'll be tripping over each other frequently."

"Does that bother you?"

"It doesn't bother me, exactly. It's just that I feel as if . . . you're encroaching on my life."

"I'm sorry," he said dryly. "I didn't realize I was intruding."

"You have a right to live your own life—"

"But you'd rather I didn't live it quite so much in your lap."

This whole thing would be much easier to do if he just wouldn't gaze at her with those piercing green eyes. "After what happened the other night, it may be . . . awkward to see so much of each other in a business setting."

"Unless we make sure it doesn't happen again?"

His voice mocked her lightly. He looked faintly cynical, as if he didn't believe a word she was saying and thought she should know better than to fling those silly words at him.

"It can't happen again," she said in a low voice.

Alexandra was being pigheaded and foolish, and Jake wanted to tell her so. But for some reason she wasn't ready to admit to the truth of how it was between them. Not yet. And if he let her go on talking to him as if she were a polite stranger, she never would.

"But it already has." He reached out, took the wineglass from her cold fingers and set it and his own on a table by the sofa. "We have only to look at each other and it happens."

She wanted to deny it—knew she must. But when he curled a hand around her neck and drew her to him as if he'd done it a hundred times before, she knew she'd been waiting for his domination from the moment she'd walked into the room. She ached to relive that easy possession, that consummate masculine confidence, that supremely sure touch—and the blinding hot sweetness that came with it.

While his caress on her nape melted her spine, he caught her hands and brought them to his chest. She breathed in sharply, her fingers tunneling into his crisp hair, as if they knew exactly what to do to please him. Deliberately, she circled her palms over the tiny buds of his nipples until they hardened and nudged against her hands.

She'd aroused him that quickly. Strength and power were hers. He'd offered himself so freely, so willingly, that an answering heat spiraled, stinging through her veins.

He muttered a word, a sigh of hunger. She groaned an answer that told him, *yes, she knew, yes she understood.*

Yes.

His hands converged on her buttocks, lifting her onto him.

His hot arousal was waiting under the towel, but it wasn't enough. She slid her hands down his ribs, found the wrapped end of the towel. Feeling as if she was stepping out onto a precipice that beckoned intolerably, she thrust her fingers between Jake's bare flesh and the terry cloth until it loosened and slid to the floor. He was naked in her arms, the way she wanted him to be.

"I knew you'd be like this," he said against her cheek. "Wild. Unafraid. As hungry as I am."

Heady, wonderful praise. Encouraged, she ran her hands up his muscled back, her throat full. He breathed a soft, "Yes, sweetheart, yes. Take whatever you want." She knew only the urge to do as he asked. She cupped his shoulders with her hands, then traced down his spine, exploring the hard indentation she'd admired so many times before.

He buried his mouth in her throat, holding her as if she were the sun and moon to him. Hunger such as she'd never known welled up in her. She'd wanted to be held just like this, in just this way ever since she could remember, by a man who could be passionate and tender all at once, by a man who, even though heat and hunger were running rampant through him, held her with such exquisite tenderness that she knew he'd never hurt her.

"Undo your buttons, sweetheart."

He let go of her a bit so she could reach the front of her blouse, but he kept his hands on her buttocks, cradling her hips into his, locking his hardness against her softness to show her how well they fit together. It was nearly unbearable, to know so much and yet not know. Unsteadily, she undid one wet buttonhole, then the next and the next. The cotton was wet and clinging, but she managed to unfasten them all.

His eyes locked with hers, dark with pleasure, waiting. She slipped her arms out of her blouse and let it slide down her back. His mouth curved in a sensuous smile, he leaned forward and kissed her bare, wet shoulder. But when he lifted his head, his green eyes gleamed. "Again," he said huskily.

She reached behind her back to unclasp her bra. When it gave, he leaned forward and used his mouth to guide one strap over her shoulder then the other.

"Get rid of it," he asked urgently.

She complied with his request.

The candlelight wavered, and in the soft light, his eyes wandered over her. He leaned down and kissed the tiny mark that still lingered on her flesh. "Mine," he whispered and took her nipple into his mouth.

The feeling of Jake's mouth on her breast was like a seductive repetition of that night by the ocean—achingly real, like a part of her that had been lost and was now returned. He lifted his mouth from her sleek, hot flesh and she cried out in need.

"Shh," he said gently, his finger on her lips. He swung her up in his arms and carried her to the couch. Smooth cool satiny material brought her briefly back to her senses. "Jake, we can't. Not here—"

He knelt on the floor and bent over her, covering her mouth with his, his hand stroking up her thigh. "We can," he murmured against her hot skin. "Mother won't come back as long as you're here. She knows better." He found the zipper of her slacks, dealt with the fastener and flattened his palm on her abdomen, his fingers reaching for her. She made a small sound of protest that turned into a cry of pleasure as he found the most sensitive part of her anatomy. Suddenly an alarm sounded through the house—foreign—jarring Alexandra to the bone.

"What is that?"

Jake muttered a dark, heartfelt curse. "My pocket pager. The storm must have knocked out the telephone."

The signal that called Jake back to the real world. When he went into the other room to turn it off, Alexandra sat up, chilled. The ability to think came flooding back, and with it cold logic.

He came back out pulling on his pants, his shirt in his hand, his bare chest evocatively masculine in the candlelight. "If I can't find a working phone, I'll have to go to the hospital."

"It's all right. I understand." And she did.

He uttered another word of frustration, but he was gentle when he leaned over and kissed her forehead. "Now you know what being with a doctor is like."

"Yes," she said hollowly.

"I'll take a rain check," he said, casually certain of her agreement.

She stood, and with as much dignity as she could muster, she brushed past him and collected her blouse and bra. Clutching her clothes in front of her, she turned to him. "There won't be any rain check."

He took a step toward her. "Sweetheart, I know this is damned inconvenient, but it isn't the end of the world. There will be other times for us—"

"No." She turned her back to him and slipped into her bra, trying to fasten it. She struggled valiantly, but it was Jake who finally stepped up and closed the fastener. While she fought with her still rioting senses that homed in on his touch, he took her blouse and held it for her.

She felt his hair brush her cheek, his mouth taste her nape. She steeled herself not to move away from this one last tender caress.

Then she turned. "It won't work, Jake. I . . . don't do well with dedicated men. I . . . forgot that for a little while. I'm glad I was reminded before . . . I went too far."

"What the hell are you talking about?"

"You can't stand around talking to me. There isn't time. You're needed, Jake. You must go. And so must I."

"You'll come back." His voice was dark with anguish. "You've got to come back."

"No," she said, and meant it.

5

HE DIDN'T GO NEAR HER. For a whole week and part of another, for long, endless days, Jake used admirable control and stayed away from Alexandra, even shunning the regular Sunday night pizza party. He waited until his free Thursday rolled around, and then sat on the patio in the morning sun, cooling his heels until he was reasonably certain he'd catch Alexandra on her lunch hour. By that time Jake was as impatient as a thoroughbred racehorse anticipating the sound of the opening gun at the gate.

On his way to see her, he told himself he wasn't going to ask her for an explanation. He didn't need that. From what little she'd said, his gut instinct told him the double whammy of Alexandra's workaholic father and a politically ambitious ex-husband had convinced her she couldn't pay the emotional price of loving a man whose career was as demanding as theirs had been.

Was she crazy, or was he? Was she right and he wrong? Maybe it was insanity to think they could successfully mesh two demanding lives like theirs. But when he remembered the way she felt in his arms and the way she made him feel, and he thought of never again knowing that blinding heat, he knew he couldn't let her drift away from him.

That was the reason why on Thursday at precisely 12:06 p.m., Jake entered Alexandra's high-rise building and stepped into the elevator that would take him up to her office.

On the ninth floor a lovely young woman whose name plate read Lea Kettavong made a serious attempt to stop him. Her determination was no match for Jake's. When he flashed a smile at her and said, "Ms. Holden is expecting me for lunch," she seemed startled. While she gazed at him with serious, puzzled eyes, trying to decide what to do, he made it easy for her by opening the door and striding through to the inner sanctum.

Alexandra was alone, but she was on the phone. When she looked up, her eyes darkened, but all she did was watch as he nodded to her and stepped politely to the window behind her back to wait until she finished her conversation.

There was a silence, and then he heard her saying, "Excuse me. I'm terribly sorry, but I've just had an . . . unavoidable interruption here. May I call you back later this afternoon, say around three? Fine. I do apologize . . . Yes, of course. Have a good lunch."

The phone settled into the cradle and she swiveled around in her chair to face him. "This is an unexpected . . . pleasure."

She looked quite at home in her high-backed leather chair, and dressed in her linen suit of kelly green with a blouse in a lighter shade that made her eyes look ocean-blue. Her brown-blond hair was immaculately arranged as usual, piled up on top of her head in a sophisticated style he didn't particularly like.

Beautiful as ever, but under a strain, he decided as he cast his practiced physician's eye over her face. Her mouth was rosy with lipstick, but there was tension around its corners, and her eyes, though skillfully highlighted with sea-green shadow, looked tired. He was probably the only man in the world who could see those signs of vulnerability under the carefully constructed facade of the beautiful businesswoman. On her desk, a gardenia flowered in a bowl, as beautiful and vulnerable as she.

"I'm sorry to barge in on you this way," he said, casually folding his arms over his chest.

"No, you're not. You're pleased with yourself that you managed to slip past Lea."

He nodded, his lips quirking, giving her the first point.

Warming up to the fight, Alexandra went on the offensive. "What lie did you tell her—that we were having lunch together?"

"Aren't we?"

"No."

"Going to toss me out?" he asked. The beginning of a smile tilted his lips. He was the daredevil male inviting the female to initiate a confrontation that he was sure of winning.

In a consummately natural gesture, she turned her executive chair toward him, leaned back and pressed her hands into her pockets. Her legs were crossed, her short skirt riding up above her knees, exposing very nice legs.

"No."

"What are you going to do?"

She rose and crossed to the window to stand a few feet away from him. Taking her hands out of her pockets, she folded her arms, whether in a conscious or unconscious imitation of him, he didn't know, and deliberately faced him. Not a shred of the memory of the passion they'd shared showed in her eyes. He may as well have been a stranger. "I'm going to wait for you to state your business."

The vulnerability he'd glimpsed was gone. She'd regrouped and marshaled her forces, rebuilt her walls. She wasn't the open-faced, openhearted young girl he'd once known.

He realized suddenly he didn't want an openhearted young girl. He liked the grown-up version much better. This sophisticated woman with her determined control, wearing the trappings of power and authority, excited him more than the girl ever had.

He knew what it cost her to stand at the top of the heap, figuratively and literally. It had cost her heartbreak and long hours and staying up nights worrying, just as his career had cost him the same. They were exactly alike, he and she. She was his equal—a woman he could respect. A woman worth fighting for.

He wandered away from her, ostensibly to examine her artwork hanging on the wall to the right of him. "Nice place you've got here."

"Thank you."

So polite, so correct, so damned—patient. He wanted to shake her. But that was not the way the game was won. "Are those paintings Creighton's?" he inquired, his back to her.

"No."

He was getting nowhere fast. Somebody had to break the ice, and it would have to be him. He swiveled around to her, aware of her eyes flaring in surprise. He had her off balance. It was now or never. "Alex, you can relax. I'm not here to make a nuisance of myself. You've said no, so as far as I'm concerned, that's that. A gentleman respects a lady's wishes, all the more when they've been friends as long as you and I have. That's why I came here to see you, so we could conduct this conversation in business surroundings where we can keep things . . . cool."

He was telling her the truth—almost—but he felt uncomfortable hedging with someone who knew him as well as she did. He kept watching her face, trying to gauge her reaction. In the silence that followed, there seemed to be none. She was a skilled player. He was up against the best.

"Do you honestly mean that?"

She wanted to believe him, he could see that. But her sixth sense and her longtime knowledge of him was making her wary. And smart. "Yes," he said, forcing his eyes to meet hers without flickering away.

"Then what do we have to talk about?" she asked reasonably.

He shrugged his shoulders, looking like a man who felt silly saying what he was about to say. "I wondered if we could work out a way to see each other in the company of our families. I'll be moving out of my mother's house eventually, but I don't have time to look for my own place until I get my office resettled. Until then, I find it awkward to keep coming up with excuses to my mother about why I can't join her when she goes to your house, or why I won't be home when you're coming to dinner." He paused. It was weak and he knew it. He'd decided to save his strongest argument for last. "It's also occurred to me that since our . . . estrangement, I haven't seen as much of Katherine as I'd like."

He was talking too damned much, using too many words. But Alexandra turned back to the window, away from him. The look on her face told him he'd struck home.

"I've been . . . sorry about that," she said softly. "It would be good for her to have a father figure in her life."

Determined to play it light, he made a sound in his throat and pulled a mocking face at her back. "Give me a break, Alex. I'm not ready for fatherhood. I was thinking more in terms of being her big brother."

She swung around to him. "I think she's missed you. Even though she wasn't receptive to you when you were around, now that you're gone, she misses having a male . . . irritant in her life."

His smile was rueful. "Nice to know I have some use, even if it's only as the grain of sand for the pearl in the oyster." He wanted to say, *And how about you? Do you miss having a male irritant in your life?* But he was smarter than that and he knew Alex better than that. If he was to foster the illusion in her that he'd given up the idea of becoming her lover, he'd have to play it to the hilt. He'd have to be so good in the role, he'd even convince himself that he didn't want her. An Academy Award performance. Unfortunately, he wasn't that good an actor.

"I sold my sailboat up North rather than tow it down here, and I've been looking for something bigger as a replacement. I've found an O'Day I like—but until I get an extension for the tiller, I'd need help to take it out. If I buy it, can I count on Katherine, or you, when she isn't available, to crew?" He put on his best doctor's noncommital expression, appearing only mildly interested in her answer.

She thought for a moment and then said, "I'll talk to her about it and let you know." When she saw the look in his eyes, she added quickly, "I'm not hedging, Jake. It's just that I can't speak for her because I don't know if she's prone to seasickness or not, and I—"

"You don't know? You mean in the two years she's been here, she's never been out in a boat?"

"I haven't had time to take her out, and Mother really isn't capable—"

"You haven't been out on the water in two years, either?"

She made a gesture with her hand that encompassed her desk and the papers scattered over it. "I haven't had much time for leisure activities lately."

He let the silence build, let her think about what she'd said. Then, with just the right soft emphasis, he murmured, "Such . . . dedication."

That was Jake's most lethal attraction, Alexandra thought, as she stood alone in her office after he'd left, staring out the window with her hands clamped to her sides. He showed her exactly who and what she was, and he did it without censure. After he'd gently pointed out that she was the pot calling the kettle black, that she had as demanding a career as he did, he'd gone. And left her standing at the window with a sick feeling in the pit of her stomach that when she'd relegated Jake from lover to friend, she'd made the biggest mistake of her life.

THE WEEK AFTER Jake vacated his office, Alexandra sold the property to the developer. With all the wheels now in motion, she immersed herself in preparation for her company's investment of capital in the Hawaiian hotel merger. This would be the ultimate success of her career as an entrepreneur and she should have been ecstatically happy. Instead, she found herself wondering when or if Jake would buy his boat and when or if she would go out in it with him. If she only went sailing when Katherine was along, she would surely be safe. Not from Jake, from herself. Safe from her restlessness, her need, her hunger.

He'd aroused her twice and he'd done it well. While her mind worked to help her forget, her body feverishly relived the ecstasy she'd felt under Jake's hands and mouth. She was almost thirty-five, something her body reminded her of on dark hot nights when she'd worked until she was exhausted and still couldn't sleep. Was this really the way she wanted to live the rest of her life? Didn't she want a man? Didn't she want a child?

She did want a man. But not just any man. A man with green eyes and a devilish smile and an easy way of moving. She did want a child. But not just any child. A child with green eyes and a devilish smile and an easy way of moving. The child she could never have.

THE NEXT SUNDAY DAWNED hot and bright, the sky so clear it hurt the eyes. Alexandra had dressed and was puttering around the house listlessly when the phone rang. Jake's voice was low in her ear, polite, almost bored. Would she and Katherine like to go out in the boat?

He sounded as if he didn't really care what the answer would be. Alexandra's ennui fell away. Nerves sparked to life, challenged by Jake's studied indifference. She put the phone to her chest and called to Katherine. The girl's lack of enthusiasm matched Jake's, but in the end she agreed to go. Alexandra put down the phone, a smile on her lips, exhilaration lifting her heart.

An hour later Jake appeared at their door. He wore an unbuttoned white shirt exposing his chest, the tails dangling over white swim trunks that skimmed his hard thighs. He looked like high summer packaged in masculinity. "The boat's all rigged and ready to go."

There was a raw quality in his voice so at odds with his casual appearance that Alexandra's nerves clenched. When he stepped inside, his face was as indifferent as his voice. He looked cold and controlled, as if it took all his effort to restrain an inner rage.

"Is something wrong?"

Jake thought he might have carried it off if he hadn't opened his mouth. She read voices like other people read books. He shouldn't have come. He wasn't fit company for anybody. But he'd needed her. So he'd asked her to do the one thing he was sure she wouldn't refuse. Looking at her only deepened the pain that had driven him to call her. She wore her hair pulled back with one of those big combs, which made her look gorgeous and hopeful and vulnerable all at the same time. His world wasn't a good place to be at the moment. He shouldn't have to look at her nice legs and smooth breasts showcased by a one-piece white swimsuit, and feel gutshot, but he did.

Seeing Jake at close range made Alexandra want to touch him. His face was stark, the skin stretched over his strong bone structure, his mouth drawn tight with control. Something was eating him from the inside. She wanted to put her fingers to that taut skin and soothe away the pain. But he was too bronzed, too hard to touch, and the dark gleam in those green depths gave him the look of a man who'd glimpsed hell and didn't want anybody looking at him too closely or they'd see it, too.

"It's nothing," he assured her.

She wasn't going to let him shut her out like that. "Tell me what's wrong."

His dark-brown lashes swept down and when they lifted, the pain had ebbed a little, as if he appreciated her persistence. "Not now. Later. I don't want to spoil Katherine's day."

Alexandra didn't want to spoil Katherine's day, either. She had no choice but to call her niece. She tried to stifle her sense of foreboding as she gathered up their things and followed Jake out the door.

On the dock he was silent, leaving it up to Alexandra to make conversation as he leaped lightly aboard the sailboat. He avoided her eyes as she handed some equipment to him—life jackets, a small cooler of soft drinks, hats. Finally, she helped Katherine come on board, his grim face making her have second thoughts about going ahead with the outing.

The boat was too small to have a cabin. It was a seventeen-footer, with a mainmast for the sail furled under the boom, rigging for a jib and a robin's egg blue foredeck. There were two long mahogany benches to sit on, room enough for them to change sides as the boat tacked, but that was all. They would be in close physical contact every minute.

What seemed like a good idea when he'd called to ask them along on his maiden voyage was becoming less so by the minute, with Jake wearing a face like stone while he bent over the small motor to start it and Katherine perched on the opposite bench, looking dully at the sky.

The small motor propelled them out of the bay beyond the jutting finger of land until they were out on the ocean proper. Jake turned off the motor and assigned Alexandra to the tiller, while he scrambled up to the front to raise the jib. Katherine sat with her chin tilted up, studying the clouds and looking withdrawn.

The wind caught the neat triangular sail and the boat began to cut through the water. Startled, Alexandra turned the tiller the wrong way.

"Into the wind," Jake directed, which meant nothing to her.

"Turn the tiller toward the sail!" he yelled, exasperated.

"The back end or the front end?"

Jake muttered something indecipherable. "The back end. Come on, Alex, you used to sail."

"A hundred years ago," she responded. "A lot of sheets have gone with the wind since then."

The tension in his face relaxed marginally. "That's the worst mixed metaphor I've ever heard."

"You might hear a few more before this trip is over."

Suddenly he grinned. Relieved, she grinned back. The world brightened. The wind filled the sail and the boat skimmed over the water. Warmed by Jake's smile, Alexandra leaned against the back of the boat and let the wind and the sun wash over her bare skin, billow the shirt she'd tossed over her swimsuit. If a real miracle happened and, by the end of the trip, Jake had gotten Katherine to smile, she would count it an astounding success.

The flap, flap of the luffing sail made Jake's smile vanish. "What in the hell are you doing?"

"The wind changed."

"That fast? Come on, Alex. You weren't holding the tiller steady."

She looked at him, sitting perched on the foredeck holding the sail steady with the rope in his hand. "You've got the easy job. Why don't you let me do that end and you take this thing?"

Jake nodded and they scrambled around, changing places. Jake had his hand on the tiller for less than a minute when the sail began to luff.

"What's the matter?" Alexandra asked.

"This wind is crazy." He sounded amazed, as if he didn't understand how Nature could play such a trick on him.

"Ha," Alexandra said.

"Ha," Katherine echoed.

He stared at them, putting on his best male-affronted expression. "What a mistake that was, bringing you two women out here to gang up on a lone, defenseless male."

"You're not defenseless," Alexandra shot back. This was more like it. Familiar ground.

"Glad you think so." Jake grinned outrageously and Katherine looked as if she was enjoying the battle of the sexes as much as the adults were.

Alexandra's heart lifted. This wasn't a mistake after all. The sheer pleasure of skimming over the ocean was beginning to work its magic on all of them. For a few enchanted moments, they had left their troubles behind them on land.

He had a mutinous, disrespectful crew, Jake said, and he'd like to conduct a court martial there and then, but he couldn't because he had to give the tiller back to Alexandra and raise the mainsail.

His eyes bright with challenge, he passed the control of the boat over to Alexandra. Her eyes gleaming with triumph, she took it.

The sail went up quickly. He involved Katherine in the process by instructing her to take a rope and lash it around a cleat. When she'd successfully secured the line under his tutelage, only Alexandra was aware of the satisfaction in his eyes as he returned to take the tiller from her.

Water swished away behind them, tumbling over and over itself in a spreading wake. Sea gulls circled, calling raucously. The sun danced off the water in a thousand sparkles. Jake leaned forward and said casually, "Second mate's turn at the tiller," and turned his green eyes on Katherine.

"No," she said instantly.

"All hands work on this ship. Stand your watch or you don't get your ration of grog."

"No, thank you." She retreated into that distant politeness that Alexandra dreaded.

To her amazement, Jake shrugged and settled back again. Don't give up so easily, she pleaded silently with him, but he stared at the sky and looked unconcerned.

"It's right you are, Katey, to keep the ship in the hands of the one competent male on board."

"You're not so competent." She rose to the bait beautifully.

He shot her a wiseacre look. "You think a mere female could do this? No. It takes skill, experience, and an instinctive feel for the wind."

"It's not that hard."

"Still, I doubt if a female, especially one of your tender age—"

The challenge dangled in the air, the gauntlet thrown down. Katherine favored him with a large helping of teenage disdain, but she was hard put to stay uninvolved, as Alexandra could clearly see.

"What if I dump us over and break up the boat?"

Jake gave her no quarter. His eyes were lowered, lazy. "You might dump us over, but you won't break us up. A sailboat's built to be righted in the water. All we'd get is wet. Then I'd extract a confession from you that the male is indeed the superior one of the species."

Several seconds of tense silence ensued. Alexandra waited, watching the girl's face—praying.

"There is no such thing as male supremacy."

"Prove it." He motioned for her to come and take the tiller. She looked torn, undecided. Just as Alexandra was certain she would shake her head no, Katherine jumped up and plopped down on the place Jake had made for her.

Watching her, Jake took his hand off the tiller. Katherine lifted her chin and slid her small hand onto the smooth mahogany stick.

Only a man who was supremely sure of himself could trust a child that much. Alexandra's heart squeezed at the thought. Jake was good for Katherine. He was good for almost everyone she knew—except herself.

Patiently Jake let Katherine make her own mistakes. She turned the boat away from the wind twice, earning herself a luffing sail. She overcorrected, making the boat tip unsteadily. Katherine quickly learned that pointing the boat into the wind was the best way to keep it upright.

"A pretty good rule is to point the tiller toward the sail," Jake said softly. "So if I change the sail direction, you change the tiller direction."

Alexandra raised an eyebrow at such rigid instructions, but said nothing. A few minutes later, when the wind changed and Jake told Katherine to turn the boat the other way, she reminded him he'd told her to point the tiller toward the sail.

"But I don't want you to do that just now," Jake said with typical male exasperation, conveniently forgetting he'd given what seemed to be an inviolable rule.

"You're a lousy teacher," Katherine said, disgusted. It was Alexandra's turn to laugh. The girl went on. "I think I should just steer by watching the sail and doing what feels right."

Jake's green eyes gleamed. "Maybe I'm not such a lousy teacher after all."

After a half hour of reasonably clear sailing, when it became apparent that Katherine had a neutral feeling for it, Alexandra suggested gently that perhaps the girl should take a break from the captaincy and have something cold to drink. Soft drink tops were snapped, and they all sat back with a cool can in their hands, each of them enjoying the freedom of skimming the green water with a sail and their skill.

"This is the one place left in the world where your destiny is in your own hands," said Jake.

Alexandra felt too lazy, too sated with sun and wind and contentment to reply. Whatever had been bothering Jake wasn't bothering him now. He sat opposite her, his long legs crossed and elegant, his bare feet propped on the bench next to her. His hair was windswept into coffee-brown tendrils, his throat exposed as he lifted his head to drink. He was bronzed and sleek and relaxed—a different man than the one who'd stood outside her door an hour ago and looked as if he was furious with the world and everything in it. Her eyes narrowed slightly, as she pondered the cause of his former black mood. Jake had always been able to cover up his thoughts. But she would find out what was wrong. Later.

Her eyes shifted to Katherine, found Katherine studying her, openly assessing her. Their eyes met and there was something in Katherine's, a look of speculation that was strangely adult. She looked as if she was wondering about Alexandra's relationship with Jake, wondering with a child's curiosity and a young woman's knowledge of the facts of life. Before Alexandra could acknowledge her perspicacity with a knowing look of her own that would neither deny nor confirm, Katherine's gaze shifted to the sky over Alexandra's shoulder.

Glimpses. That was what was so frustrating. She'd get glimpses of emotion, glimmers of feeling. But before she could act on them, Katherine had rebuilt the wall.

She'd lowered it for Jake. Not once, but twice. Maybe if Jake went on as he was, she would get into the habit. Alexandra tried not to think of what it would be like to see Katherine laughing and smiling as other girls her age did. She'd wanted that for so long and had almost decided it was too much to hope for.

A big black-striped machine that looked more like a race car than a motorboat thundered by, churning up the water, making the sailboat bob crazily and the sails fold and creak. Jake muttered an angry word, his eyes dark as he stared after the offending boat. The people in it were laughing and talking, unaware they'd come too close to an unpowered boat and had made it wobble in their wake.

"So much for being the captain of my destiny. It's getting too crowded out here. We'd better head in."

Jake pulled the sailboat up to the dock. With a wise look over her shoulder at her aunt, Katherine sauntered ahead of them and went on to the house, leaving Alexandra alone with Jake.

While she waited, he took his time mooring the boat, wrapping the rope around the post enough times to keep it safe through a hurricane. At last he straightened lithely and faced her, as if he knew what she was going to say.

"I want to know what's bothering you."

He squinted into the sun. She shuffled through the things she held and unearthed his sunglasses.

His gaze, direct, indulgent, shifted back to her. "Nosy old lady, aren't you?" He took the sunglasses, a smile a woman would die for on his lips.

"Nosy, yes—lady, yes—old, no. Don't try any of your fancy sidestepping on me. What's the matter?"

He lifted a fist and laid it lightly against her jaw in a mock hit that was more caress than threat. "Since you're such a tender young thing, I'll have to wait until you're older to tell you all my deep, dark secrets." She opened her mouth to protest but like lightning sizzling through the sky, the pain returned to his eyes. "If you keep on, you're going to spoil my day," he said lightly.

She had already started to say something. "Jake—" She reached out and wrapped her fingers around his arm. He was hard, warm, vibrant. But he flinched as if she'd shot him.

"Dammit, woman, I've already got one mother. I don't need two." With an agile grace, he stepped around her and strode down the dock, leaving her to stare after him with anxious frustration.

Jake had shut her out. She couldn't remember the last time that had happened—or the last time she'd been quite so worried about him.

In her bedroom, she stripped off her suit, stepped into her shower and turned the cold water on full force. Anything to keep from thinking that she should have stood right there and insisted he tell her what was wrong. But her questions had brought the pain back to his eyes and she'd backed off, unable to bear the thought that she was making him hurt.

That evening, she waited with anxious anticipation to see if he would follow Helen in the door for their Sunday night supper. When he didn't, she quizzed his mother and got a very unsatisfactory response.

"I think he's tired. He's been working too hard, poor dear."

Helen's eyes flickered away from Alexandra's. Jake was more than tired and they both knew it.

"Has he gone to bed? I'd like to see him, but if he's resting—"

"Why no, dear, he wasn't in bed when I left. I believe he was reading."

Alexandra couldn't get Jake to answer her rap at the sliding glass door. Without a flicker of guilt, she opened it and stepped in. He was sitting in a chair in the living room, uncharacteristically still, his long legs stretched out in front of him. He wore the same clothes he had on that afternoon.

He stared at her, his face bare of any reaction to her presence. In the heat of the late afternoon, he looked cold. His hair was more dishevelled than it had been in the boat, his eyes expressionless. "What do you want?"

It wasn't a welcoming opening. "I came over to see what you were doing and why you didn't come over to eat with us."

"I wasn't hungry."

"Why not?" she asked lightly.

He looked at her then, and there was stark coldness in his eyes—an utter lack of feeling. "I didn't want to spend any more time looking at you. I still don't. So get the hell out."

His words stung. At sixteen, he'd have devastated her with such a blunt dismissal. But she wasn't sixteen. She took another step into the room. "I want to know what's the matter with you. And I'm not leaving until you tell me."

He examined her like a surgeon trying to decide where to place the knife. "You like beauty, Alex, and you're a patron of the arts. You'd like Yosheko. He's a beautiful, eleven-year-old Japanese-American boy. His hands are beautiful. The music he makes on a violin is beautiful." He looked away from her, past her shoulder. "He has leukemia. He was in remission until yesterday." His eyes came back, found hers, fastened on them. "He's fighting with every bit of courage in his beautiful soul, but he's losing. There just aren't any more damned miracles to be had."

"I'm . . . sorry." Such inept words.

"So am I." A deep, despairing irony laced his words.

"Is there . . . anything I can do for you?"

His green eyes roved over her. "You just spent the morning acting like a jolly good pal. That's probably enough for one day."

"Jake, I—" She took a step toward him.

"You weren't going to get involved with me, remember? Something about the pressures of my career, I believe." His eyes were like bits of green glass. "You were smarter than you knew. Stay smart, Alex. Leave me alone in my private hell. It isn't a place I want to share with anybody. . . least of all you."

6

PRIDE. Jake had an incredible amount of pride. Those who didn't know him might not see how it radiated from every lift of his head, every movement of his shoulders under the elegant tuxedo, every lift of his sensual, disciplined mouth.

Alexandra could see it. Under the brilliant chandelier of The Cotillion—the dining place of the rich, beautiful and ambitious of the Florida Keys—she sat three tables away from Jake. But every time he turned his head to talk to his dinner companion, the woman he'd escorted to the Chamber of Commerce dinner dance, the turn of his head caught Alexandra's eye.

She was hungry for the sight of him. Two weeks after the night he'd told her about his young patient, he'd moved out of his mother's house and into his condo. There were no more pleasant jogs together, no more looking over and seeing Jake lounging on the patio, no more shared Sunday night pizzas. The sun rose over an empty beach and so did the moon.

It was what she had wanted. It made everything simpler. Now there was no need to concoct excuses to avoid Helen, or to stay indoors when she would rather have been out lounging on the beach. The beach was empty. Which made her life much easier. Or did it just make it emptier?

Jake leaned back in his chair, his brown hair shimmering under the light, a smile on his mouth that might have been tolerant, amused, sensual, or all three. Alexandra lifted food to her mouth, paying no attention to what she had scooped onto her fork. Mashed potatoes. She loathed mashed potatoes. That she had actually put mashed potatoes inside her mouth proved she was in no fit state to be allowed out. She chewed and tried to swallow, not a pleasant task.

Ted Mannahan sat on her right. He was a lawyer, a married man with three children. His wife had foregone the dance to remain at home with her brood, sending Ted on alone.

Alexandra liked Ted. He hadn't done any work for her firm, but she'd decided that if she and Doug Concannon ever parted company, Ted would be her choice for legal counsel. Even in his tuxedo, the man managed to look disheveled. His untidy look lulled unsuspecting folk into dropping their guard. Just when he had them convinced he was just about smart enough to find his way home, they discovered they had told him all their secrets.

"Nice party," he drawled, as the waiter was removing their plates. When the young man hesitated at taking Alexandra's because most of the prime rib, potatoes and broccoli remained, she shook her head, indicating for him to take it away.

"Good food," said Ted.

"Yes," Alexandra agreed, smiling brightly. "How are your children?"

"My oldest is flunking out of school—"

Alexandra tried to listen, but her attention was split. Her eyes were drawn to Jake as he bent his head forward to hear what his companion was saying. The woman, bronze-skinned with the flowing black hair of an island beauty, leaned over and whispered into his ear. Jake's face split into one of his most endearing grins. It hurt more than Alexandra thought it possibly could to see the woman's face light up in response. During the last few weeks, Jake had flashed his grins only at her. That had seemed right. Watching his magic work so effectively on another woman seemed all wrong.

". . . my daughter broke her leg water-skiing . . ."

Alexandra wasn't jealous, of course she wasn't. She could never be dog in the manger about Jake. She was happy that he had found feminine companionship. True—the woman's nose was a little long and her front teeth were a bit crooked, but what did a few minor flaws matter? She seemed friendly, warm, charming.

The woman leaned a curved, bare shoulder close to Jake, brushing his.

Too darn warm, friendly, and charming.

". . . youngest is turning into a holy terror. He's driving my wife to drink."

Ted's calm, impersonal tone gave Alexandra the clue for her response. "I'm glad they're all well."

"I thought you would be," Ted murmured. "Why don't you go over and tear her hair out?"

He had Alexandra's attention then. She turned silvery blue eyes on Ted, aware that she'd been caught, but valiantly pretending she didn't have the vaguest idea what he was talking about. "Tear whose hair out?"

He nodded toward Jake. "Her name is Amanda Newton. She's one of those rare specimens, a Keys native. Does secretarial work for a contractor." His keen brown eyes watched and waited.

She tried to face him down with a bluff. "You're a dangerous man to be running around loose, counselor."

He grinned, looking pleased at her recognition of his alter ego. Alexandra suspected Superman had been his favorite hero. Or the Scarlet Pimpernel.

"You can always file an appeal."

She shook her head. "The case has been thrown out for lack of evidence."

"Too bad," Ted murmured thoughtfully, shifting his eyes to Jake. "Rumor had it you two were an item."

"Rumor was just that. Rumor."

Out of the habit of listening subconsciously in executive meetings and replaying in her head what she'd heard, Ted's statements about his family floated to the surface. A rueful smile curved Alexandra'a lips. "I'd like to send your daughter flowers. What hospital is she in?"

Ted threw his head back and laughed. "Gotcha."

"Didn't you just," she murmured, smiling.

Jake's eyes flickered over to Alexandra. Her smile was as lovely as ever and there was a faint pink flush coloring her cheeks. He was glad she was enjoying herself. She had a right to enjoy herself. But did she have to look so damn beautiful while she did it? Her shoulders were all the more enticing for the tiny black straps curved over them. She'd done something different with her hair to make it look exotic for an evening out, all swooped up on one side, baring one elegant cheekbone. There were other elegant bones that were bare, her collarbone, her elbows, her wrist bones. She wore no bracelets and only one tiny gold signet ring on her right pinkie finger, a gift from Katherine last Christmas that had been too small to wear on her ring finger.

He knew the guy she was talking to. He was married, with a family. Jake had treated one of the kids for sore throat recently. He supposed from Alexandra's viewpoint, the guy was safe. He looked about as safe as a man-eating shark at the moment. He'd be lucky if he didn't find Jake's fist on his sweet-talking mouth before the night was over.

The interminable meal ended just a few minutes after Jake decided he'd acted like a prize fool inviting Amanda to the dinner dance. It had seemed like a good idea at the time. She'd come into the office with her little boy. She'd told Jake that she was recently divorced and that she didn't want to get involved with anyone, but she would really like to meet some new people. She was pleasant, a good conversationalist, easy on the eyes and liked to dance. She'd seemed ideal.

Jake liked a good band. He liked a generous dance floor. The Cotillion had both. What he didn't like was seeing Alexandra move around it in the arms of that grinning idiot. Dammit, the man was barely as tall as she was, and he looked like an unmade bed. Did women automatically fall for that little-boy tousled look? He'd like to give him a shiner to complete that picture of all-American boy.

Amanda had excused herself to go to the powder room. Had she sensed his distraction? He hoped not. Only a damn fool of a man invited one woman out while he ached for another one. But he'd done exactly that. Which made him the biggest damn fool of all.

Determined to redeem himself, he turned his head away from the dance floor, propped his elbow on the little round table in front of him and waited for Amanda to return.

When she walked back toward him, he smiled and invited her to dance. He had the best of intentions, but that wasn't enough. He was aware of her gracefulness when she slipped into his arms, but when he pulled her closer, his mind turned cool and rebellious and his body followed suit. Nothing about Amanda was right. Her scent, the way she fit into his arms, the way she moved with him was all wrong.

When they left the dance floor, she turned to him, her eyes meeting his. "I know it's early, but I think I'd better be going. The sitter's new and I hate to leave her with my son for too long."

"Of course," said Jake politely, picking up her stole to hold it for her, feeling like a heel.

They were leaving. It was barely ten o'clock and Jake was helping the woman with her wrap. Nerves tightened in Alexandra's stomach.

"Is something wrong?" Ted asked.

"No. I . . . yes. I'd like to go back and sit down if you don't mind."

Gently, Ted guided her back to their table. "You should have eaten more for dinner. Would you like a drink? Something nonalcoholic?"

"Yes. Coffee, I think."

His eyes sympathetic, he signaled the waitress.

An hour later, Alexandra drove home slowly, the nausea lying just under the surface of her consciousness. Both houses were dark when she pulled up in front of hers. Slowly, she made her way up the stairs. The penlight attached to her key chain afforded some light while she unlocked the door.

Inside her bedroom, she stood in the dark, feeling the softness of the night air pouring in her window. She felt caught, intolerably caught. She wanted to be safe. She'd worked so hard to be safe. For two long years, she'd struggled to exorcise the dream of being loved completely, irrevocably, unendingly. It was an impossible dream. There was no such love. At least, not from the men she picked. A man whose most serious thoughts centered around catching a stringer of fish off the Seven Mile bridge might satisfy her need for an uncomplicated relationship. But she couldn't imagine loving such a man.

Maybe it went deeper than that. Maybe she chose inappropriate men to love because she didn't really want to love. Maybe she was afraid of the vulnerability loving and being loved demanded. To be totally naked, totally vulnerable, totally wanting with a man she loved was something she'd never done. It required trust.

She didn't trust, not since her father showed her how much trusting could hurt. Jake might have taught her how to trust, but fate had removed him from her life before he had the chance. Now fate had tossed Jake back at her and this time, it was she, not fate, who hadn't given him the chance.

The strength to be naked and vulnerable. That was what she needed. She walked to the window and looked out at the sea. In all the years she'd lived beside the water, both as a teenager and as an adult, she'd never gone swimming in the nude. She'd never had the courage to be that crazy, that wild, that sensitive to the elements. She was almost thirty-five years old. When would she have the courage?

She'd always been the responsible, mature adult, never giving in to the child in her, never having the courage to play like a child, the way Jake had that first day in the surf.

She needed to go looking for the child in her. The child she'd never been.

Moving slowly, as if she had all the time in the world, she began to undress.

Outside in the heated darkness, she stood beside the ocean, her body wrapped in a towel. The sand was warm on her bare feet, the breeze cool. The water glistened in the dark, a vast shimmering mirror, inviting her in. She dropped the towel and walked forward into the water, savoring the coolness swirling around her bare thighs, her hips, her breasts.

He should have called out to her, let her know he was there. He should have risen out of the shadows of the patio and warned her of his presence. He would have, but it didn't seem important. It seemed an impertinence to intrude on her privacy.

There was no way he could have guessed that when she dropped the towel he would see her slim naked body silvered by the moon. He hadn't known Alexandra had the desire—or the courage—to slip naked into the primitive allure of the sea.

The ocean bubbled over her shoulders as if welcoming a friend, night-cool, sleek as silk on her skin. But unlike silk, the water didn't constrict, confine, or trap. It slid over her, blanketing her from the moon's bright rays, cradling her with the gentleness of the womb. She slipped through the water with the ease of a seal.

As she swam, she discovered some of life's anomalies, that in darkness there is light, in coolness there is warmth—and in vulnerability there is strength. She swam on, stripping away layers of pride, and of lies, until all that was left was her essence, burning inside of her.

He watched her slow, patient stroking as she swam parallel to the shore, the slant of her slim pale arms above the gleaming darkness of the water. She was breaking all the rules, swimming alone and at night, but his deep understanding of her told him there was more to her midnight swim than the simple need for exercise. It was a witch's ritual, an affirmation of life and all that was both real and magical in the night world. She'd become one with the stars, the sea, the small cloud drifting across the face of the moon, the palm trees that rustled to her in night whispers. She was both their captive—and their mistress.

He sat there watching her slow, paced swimming far longer, it seemed, than she should have stayed in the water, long enough to make him feel cramped and chilled as he sat waiting. But at last, her water-shadowed head turned and she was upright, wading ashore through the shallow water, her slim body gleaming wet and silvery in the moonlight, her smooth thighs dripping water.

She leaned down for the towel, and with a grace that made his throat constrict, she wrapped it around her bent head and straightened. With her breasts high and peaked from the cold water, her shoulders silver in the moonlight, her long, lean flanks wet with sea water, she walked into the night as she had into the sea, naked, beautiful—alone.

Before, when he'd watched her go into the water, shock and a deep sense of awe had kept his body from reacting. He had no such protection now. Desire rose, hot and heavy in his throat, choking him, spreading to his loins like a brushfire. Even more insistent was the need to share—and shatter—her loneliness. He was seeing Alexandra as no man, no one, had ever seen her—alone, courageous, vulnerable. So vulnerable that it hurt to look at her.

He had never been more proud of her.

An instinctive age-old wisdom told him to stay in the shadows. He sat still, his heart pounding. She would never forgive him for intruding on her privacy. He would never forgive himself for intruding on the utterly pagan beauty of her nakedness. The roll of her hips and the smooth movement of her buttocks was the last glimpse he had of her as she disappeared onto her patio.

Alexandra refused to wrap herself in the towel, even when she stepped inside the house and the coolness of the air conditioning hit her wet skin. Her feet sandy, her head high, she walked into her bedroom. Only when she stepped under the hot spray of the shower, did she feel the strange spell that had gripped her slipping away.

ON THE FOLLOWING Saturday morning, Alexandra was food shopping with Katherine in the biggest grocery store in Marathon. She was frowning over the selection of lettuce when she turned and nearly ran head on into Jake, who was frowning over the cauliflower heads.

He was too close. Fruit and vegetable smells were preempted by the clean scent of Jake's skin. She felt the faint uneasiness that always accompanied Jake's presence and the resulting overload of stimuli to her senses.

She could see too much, feel too much. There was a tiny nick in his chin where he'd cut himself shaving. His chinos were crisp and so was the knit shirt that he wore open at the throat. His tan was the darkest she'd ever seen on him. In his deep coppery-brown face, his eyes looked even more like emeralds glittering in the sun. He'd obviously been spending time on the beach despite his heavy work schedule. With the vivacious Amanda, perhaps.

Of course, she was in old khaki shorts she'd dragged from the drawer, and her hair was Saturday casual.

"Hello," he said.

Incredible. She'd forgotten how the sound of his voice made her skin dance. She lifted her chin. "Hello, Jake."

He spoke to Katherine just as politely. The girl's eyes flared darkly with some emotion—anger?—before she responded with a clipped "hi."

Katherine's reception seemed to bother him. His eyes flickered over her. "How's my favorite second mate?"

"Fine." Katherine gave no quarter.

Jake tried another tack. His gaze returned to Alexandra. "And Beatrice? Is she well?"

"She's fine," Alexandra said, wishing she could find a graceful way to end this futile exercise in uttering polite clichés.

He appeared unmoved by the pervasive tension. He leaned back on his basket and his mouth quirked fractionally as if he'd just had an amusing thought. "She's recovered from losing the battle for a new patio, then." His gaze caught and held Alexandra's. "Was it very hard to tell her no?"

"'One small step for a woman . . .'" she murmured.

Jake smiled one of his uninhibited smiles, the kind that made Alexandra feel as if the earth had shifted a degree under her feet. "One giant step for the independence of womankind."

She didn't want to remember the discussion she'd had with Jake about her inability to tell her mother no, or tell him about her newfound strength to do just that. She didn't want to see him smile with understanding. She didn't want to feel as if he was the only man who had ever understood her. She cast about for another topic of conversation and in desperation, glanced down at his basket. Two Cornish game hens were piled on top of each other, along with one bottle of rosée wine, a box of wild rice, and two small cheesecakes plucked from the bakery counter. Dinner for two.

"I'd better not keep you," she said.

"I'm not in any hurry."

His voice was casual, but his eyes taunted her. He'd noticed her cataloging the contents of his basket, and watched her arrive at her conclusion. The darned man was a mind reader. Or maybe he just knew her too well. What would happen if she took the war into the enemy camp with all flags flying? "It looks as if you're expecting company."

"Not company exactly. My associate agreed to take his life in his hands and let me cook dinner tonight."

"Brave man." Alexandra was amazed at how easy it was to smile at Jake just then.

"You don't know the half of it," he murmured.

Katherine made a restless movement, an unspoken request to leave. Alexandra knew that's what she should do. "I didn't know you had an associate."

His eyes caught hers, held them with their darkness, their greenness—their honesty. "I intended to mention it to you a couple of times, but...the opportunity never arose." Each word was loaded with meaning, and his eyes were dark with the memory of the night they'd almost made love. He would have told her that night—if she hadn't been so eager to walk away from him.

His eyelids swept down, shuttering the dark look. "If you'd care to take your life in your hands, I'll throw in an extra bird and you can join us for dinner."

Take her life in her hands. She'd be doing exactly that. Yet, since that night on the beach when she'd come to terms with who she really was, it had occurred to her that there were worse things than being disappointed in love. There was cowardice. And loneliness.

She wanted to say so many things to him. This wasn't the right place or the right time, nor did she want to try to tell him how much her feelings had changed in front of his colleague. Perhaps Jake had invited her to dinner because another man would be present. He might not even be interested in her change of heart. He and his lovely lady might be doing just fine, thank you. She might be too late.

"I'd rather risk my life...another time."

Bleakness shuttered his face. Just when she'd needed him to understand her the most, his mind reading abilities had failed him. She'd hurt him. And destroyed her chance of reclaiming what they'd nearly had.

"Yes, of course." Polite, cool and utterly disbelieving.

"Excuse me." A woman, her brows drawn together in front, cast them an exasperated look. "If you don't mind, I'd like to look at the lettuce."

"I am sorry," Alexandra responded, moving away from Jake as she shifted to one side of the aisle. Suddenly, she was a million miles away from him—and he from her.

"I guess we'd better go. It was good to see you again." For once, the cliché meant exactly what it was supposed to mean.

"You, too," Jake said just as politely.

Alexandra caught a glimpse of his eyes as she wheeled her cart around, and she wished she hadn't. He looked so remote—and disappointed in her. Inside her head a small voice laughed mockingly. Jake couldn't be as disappointed in her as she was in herself.

All her fine resolutions to change had wilted there among the lettuce. After her nocturnal swim she had been courageous, at least for a little while. But when the crunch had come, she'd reverted to form and refused Jake's invitation to dinner because it wasn't safe and she wanted it to be. One solitary, naked dip in the sea hadn't changed her. She was still a coward.

It took her most of the morning to recover from her encounter with Jake in the grocery store, most of the afternoon to convince herself that she had not made a mistake. She would see Jake soon and she would tell him . . .

Tell him what? That she was ready to take a chance? That she was ready to go to bed with him?

Now there was a topic she'd never had to prepare for presentation. How should she play it?

Casual? *Excuse me, Jake, but about that rain check . . .*

Formal? *I've done some additional research and discovered that . . .*

Or contemporary? *Hey, sailor, how about a weekend in Miami?*

That evening, Alexandra was just finishing up a light supper with her mother and Katherine when the phone rang. Beatrice rose to answer it. She returned wearing an odd look on her face, as if she were struggling not to smile. "It's for you, Katherine. It's a boy."

Katherine's face assumed a cool inscrutable look as she rose from the table and went into the kitchen to take her call. Alexandra didn't feel nearly as cool. She wasn't sure she was ready for this. She couldn't manage her own love life and now she'd have Katherine's to worry about.

When Katherine returned to the table a few moments later, her cheeks were flushed and her neck was a faint pink under her tan.

"Who was it?" Alexandra had learned a long time ago to affect casualness when she asked her niece anything personal.

Katherine shot her an eloquent look, but finally said, "His name is John Valentine. He takes a lot of flack in school because of his name and . . . other things."

"Is he nice?"

Katherine shrugged. "I guess so. He's been . . . okay."

"What did he want?"

"He wanted me to go out for ice cream with him and his brother. His brother's older and he's got a car."

The butterflies in Alexandra's stomach went into warp speed, all zooming in different directions. "What did you tell him?"

"I told him I didn't feel like it."

Braced for a different problem entirely, Alexandra was nonplussed. "Why did you tell him that?"

Katherine shot her a rebellious look. "Because it was the truth. Who needs a guy around to make you miserable?"

Totally thrown, Alexandra said, "Katherine—"

"I don't need him. I don't need anybody. They're all alike. They hang around you when they feel like it and when they don't feel like it, they split."

"Nobody's dropped you—"

"Jake did."

Alexandra froze. "That was my fault, not Jake's. We had a misunderstanding and—"

"What did that have to do with me? He didn't have to shut me out of his life, too."

"No, he didn't," Alexandra said softly, "but maybe that's what he thought he had to do. I can talk to him and—"

Katherine's color deepened. She rose from the table, her slender fingers gripping the back of the chair. "Don't do me any favors, okay? I have to be a charity case for you, but not for him." Carefully, with the dignity of a princess, she pushed in her chair and walked around the table toward the hallway to escape to her room.

In the quiet at the table, Beatrice's eyes met Alexandra's. Her mother's gaze was dark and sympathetic. "I should have tried harder to make you understand how difficult it would be to raise a young, grieving girl."

It was one of the few times in her life Alexandra felt she'd garnered her mother's undivided attention. She gathered up her napkin and laid it on the table. "Don't take the whole world's difficulties on your shoulders, Mother. It's not your fault. We took her because she's family. She belongs with us. There was no other choice.

As for her attitude, how could you have known she'd be so bitter?"

"You're a wonderful businesswoman, dear. I've always admired you for that. This . . . well, this is something else. It may take you awhile to—"

"It's been awhile. And then some. If things go on much longer like this, I'll have to get professional help for her. I just hate to admit that she needs it, I guess. I keep thinking she'll understand how much we love her, how much we want her in our lives, and that will be enough for her. Maybe it's wrong of me to feel that way. I don't know what to think, anymore."

At the end of the meal, when her mother gathered up their few dishes and insisted she could do them alone, Alexandra rose and went to the window to soothe her eyes with the familiar view of the sea. The promontory to the left was dark with summer growth. Soon Katherine would be out of school. What would she do with the girl all summer? In a few weeks, Alexandra would be immersed in the final stages of her Hawaiian hotel deal, which would culminate in a trip to the Islands. How could she leave while Katherine was still in this state of mind?

Under other circumstances, she might have called on Jake for assistance. But his aborted effort to stand in as a surrogate father had exacerbated the situation.

She'd have to talk to Katherine tonight, even though she had a briefcase full of work to do this evening. She also had planned to do a final reading of the contract, study each item and interpret the legalese to make sure it said what she wanted it to say.

If she started reading this minute, it would still take four, possibly five hours of work to finish before she went to bed. Whatever time she spent talking to Katherine, she could subtract from her hours of sleep.

If she had another futile talk with Katherine, it would be hard to concentrate on the work waiting for her. But she must be able to shift efficiently from the personal to the professional. She couldn't afford to allow her worries about Katherine to distract her from giving the contract a careful examination. True, Sarah and Concannon, her lawyer, had each been over it twice. But ultimately, it was her responsibility to see that all was in order. The merger was such a financial gamble that if she slipped up anywhere along the line, it could be disastrous for both her firm and her family.

In the coming years, she faced more financial responsibility for her family, not less. There was the possibility of high-cost health care her mother's getting older might bring, as well as Katherine's college tuition.

Alexandra wrapped her arms around her middle. She felt caught, trapped between needing all her energy to plan for her family's financial security and knowing they needed her emotional support as well. It was an old battle, one she never seemed to resolve successfully. She was only one human being with a limited level of endurance and a limited number of hours in the day.

For the first time in her life, she thought of her father and felt a flicker of understanding. Then, she headed down the hall toward Katherine's room, knowing it would be the wee small hours before she could lay her head down on her pillow.

ON MONDAY MORNING, she elected to drive a sober-faced Katherine to school herself and get into the office an hour late. They'd made some progress in their talk Saturday night, but Alexandra had the distinct feeling she was the pot calling the kettle black. How could she convince Katherine that it was better to take a chance on a relationship than live your whole life playing it safe, when that's exactly what she'd done? In the car, their conversation centered on Katherine's plea to Alexandra to promise that she wouldn't call Jake from work.

A dozen problems greeted Alexandra's arrival on the ninth floor. Sarah followed her into her office and solemnly delivered them one by one.

Hennings had phoned and wanted an immediate decision on the date of her arrival in Hawaii.

"Tell Lea to ring him back. And bring me a cup of coffee, would you please?"

Sarah returned with a steaming cup which Alexandra sipped gratefully. "Lea has Hennings on the line for you."

"Thanks, Sarah. Go on back to your office and get the routine stuff for the day ready while I talk to him." Sarah nodded and left.

Alexandra hadn't said much more than hello to Hennings when Lea came in and laid a note on her desk. Dr. Jake Hustead was on the other line and would like to speak with her before he saw his next patient. Did she have time to talk to him now, or should he call back?

She covered the receiver with her palm. "Ask him if he can hold for a few seconds." She took her hand away and studied her calendar. She needed to give Hennings a definite date for her arrival in Hawaii. By some miracle Lea had penciled in Katherine's birthday on the twenty-fifth. Silently blessing her efficient staff, she returned her attention to Hennings. "How does the 28th sound?"

"That should be all right. I'll check with the others and get back to you."

"Do that. I'll talk to you then." She said goodbye quickly and punched the line button that was blinking. "Hi."

"Hi. You're busy."

"No more than you. What can I do for you?"

Now there was a question, Jake thought, lifting an eyebrow as he leaned back in his chair. "I called you at work because I wanted you to be able to talk freely. I wondered if you could tell me why Katherine looked at me in the grocery store the other day like I was a plate of spoiled spaghetti."

Alexandra laughed. Typical of Jake to provide the one bright spot in her morning. Suddenly, she felt relaxed, good. "Because you are a plate of spoiled spaghetti?" she teased, her voice sweet.

"I get no respect."

"You get what you deserve."

There was a brief silence. "You're stalling, Alex."

What was she going to do? Where did her loyalties lie? She'd kept her promise, she hadn't called Jake. But if Katherine found out they'd discussed her . . .

The heck with it. Her loyalties lay in doing everything she could to bring Katherine back to the land of the living. The girl needed to see Jake again, whether she wanted to admit it or not. Nothing ventured, nothing gained. "She thinks you've kicked her out of your life."

There was a pause as Jake thought it over. "I can see why she may think that. Would you object if I tried to rectify the situation?"

How like him not to waste time raking over the past and blaming things on her. Her heart warmed. He really was...something special. "You do and I'll...send you roses."

Another silence. Knowing Jake as she did, she knew he was smiling.

"Make them red, and those kind that smell up the whole room, and you've got yourself a deal."

"Would you like them to come one a day like vitamins, or are you a lavish, spendthrift, dozen-at-a-time type?"

"Surprise me." Jake hung up the phone quickly before she lost her nerve—or he lost his.

THE NEXT THURSDAY AFTERNOON, on his day off, Jake sat holding the jib sheet, carefully examining the sky. Katherine perched in the stern, her hand on the tiller, her face coolly controlled. She'd said only a few perfunctory words since he'd picked her up at school as prearranged by Alexandra. He'd dropped her off at her house so she could change into her swimsuit, and had the boat ready by the time she appeared at the dock. The fact that she'd agreed to come at all was a good sign.

When they were beyond the promontory and the breeze was blowing steady and sure, Jake stopped staring at the sky and fixed his green eyes on Katherine. "You realize why I brought you out here, don't you?"

She lifted her chin, suddenly looking amazingly like her aunt. "Sure. Aunt Alex asked you to."

Alexandra had warned him. He blessed her for giving him much-needed help. "You're wrong, Katherine. I called her and asked about you."

"Why would you do that?"

"Because I care about you."

Katherine lifted her chin a notch higher and stared at the sails. "Nobody cares about me. You're just out here with me because you want to get in good with Aunt Alex."

He felt the first flare of annoyance. How cynical the young could be when they were hurting.

"If I wanted to 'get in good with Aunt Alex,'" he said in a dry drawl, "I'd damned sure find a better way of doing it than spending the afternoon with a self-pitying young girl who's got a chip on her shoulder a yard wide, and who's working hard to be the poorest company this side of Florida City."

The sail luffed, giving Jake another encouraging sign. He'd bothered her enough to interfere with her concentration. Quickly, Katherine brought the boat back into the wind. The girl did love to sail. And she had a steady hand on the tiller and an instinctive feel for command. Like her aunt.

"You're the only one who talks to me like that."

"I'm sorry—"

"Don't be. I need somebody to yell at me the way you do . . . like I was a normal rotten kid."

Jake lifted his eyebrows, and tried to clear his thoughts. This one was too bright by far. "You are a normal rotten kid. Double-dosed rotten."

"So—why bother with me? With this?" She gestured at the sailboat.

She was so prickly and defensive he wanted to shake her. "I'm a guy who likes to live on the edge," he said instead with elaborate carelessness.

"Sure." The word was packed with a wealth of skepticism. She was skepticism dressed in a pink bikini.

"And you're a challenge. I like challenges, a thousand-piece jigsaw puzzle, impossible crosswords . . ."

He felt the first twinge of exasperation. He needed another contentious female in his life like he needed hives. "And to get back to the topic of your aunt, believe me, if I wanted to get in good with her, I'd have sent her flowers. Or taken her to dinner."

"What if she wouldn't go?"

"I'd keep asking her until she'd agree. I'm a man who doesn't give up easily."

She looked at him then, and he could swear there was a ghost of a smile touching her lips. His heart lifted. She asked, "Is that macho warning for me, too?"

He grinned. "It might be—if you don't shape up."

Her eyes flickered away from him and her face turned cool and expressionless. "How can you be like that? How can you go on . . . trying with people even when they push you away?"

"Maybe because I'm pretty sure people put up fences because they want somebody to care enough to tear them down. With some people the higher their fences are, the more they need somebody to tear them down—and the more rewarding it is to discover what's behind the fence."

Katherine stared up at the sky. "I hate . . . needing people. I hate feeling like I'll die if I don't see them. I hate . . . wanting to call them on the phone. I hate feeling alive when they're around—and dead when they're gone."

"Are we talking about people in general or person in particular?"

"There's a guy at school. He's . . . different. All the other kids think he's weird because he writes poetry and draws instead of playing baseball. We talk, sometimes. He tells me I'm a jerk to feel guilty about my parents' death and a double jerk to care about what the other kids think about me."

"Nice guy," Jake murmured, his tongue only partly in his cheek.

"I know he's right, only I just can't . . . toss things off as easily as he can. I still keep wishing things were . . . different."

Jake said nothing.

Katherine studied him. "Aren't you going to tell me what's wrong?"

"Nope."

"Aren't you going to tell me anything?"

Jake considered it. "I'm here to listen, not tell."

Emotion rose swiftly and centered in her eyes. "I really do hate it when you do that to me."

"Do what?"

"Make me feel like you understand me so much I can't help but like you."

"Sorry." He smiled. "I'll take lessons from you. How to be obnoxious in ten easy lessons. As long as I get my choice of classrooms. We'll meet here, Teach." He pointed a finger down at the floor of the sailboat.

She fastened her eyes carefully on the sail. A breeze lifted a lock of her hair. She looked almost happy. "Do you think it might take you a few more lessons than ten?"

A feeling of warmth filled him. She might not know it, but her fence had come down a notch. "Could be I'm a real slow learner. It might take fifteen or twenty sessions before I really get the hang of it."

She gave him a look and he held up his hand. "I know. You don't want me to feel any obligation." He sobered then, and decided he'd better make sure this Holden female understood the ground rules before, not after, they developed a relationship. "There's always the possibility that I might have a medical emergency and have to cancel out on you, Katherine. If I do, we'll reschedule our sail for another day. You have my promise on that."

She looked at him as if he wasn't very bright. "Sure. I understand. You're a doctor. It's no big deal. I won't get all bent out of shape if some kid gets sick and needs you. We'll just do like you said. Reschedule." Then, she smiled at him, a shy lift of the lips that made his heart squeeze suddenly with an emotion he couldn't identify.

The female of the species. Capricious, puzzling, beautiful, and served up in more varieties than a mere man could imagine, much less understand.

7

IT WAS NEARLY NOON when Janet brought the narrow, half-size florist box into Jake's office, put it down carefully on his desk and stood back with arms folded, waiting for him to open it.

Jake knew it would be the promised rose from Alex. A day brightener. He needed one. He'd seen Yosheko this morning. The boy was holding his own, but not much more. He'd watched the boy walk out of his office, wondering about the cruelty of hoping, the cruelty of life, the cruelty of having a colossal talent that would never have the chance to mature.

Janet cleared her throat. She wasn't going to leave until she saw what was inside the box. He tried to keep a cool face and not look like a kid on Christmas morning when he untied the red bow, lifted the lid and pulled back the green tissue paper to discover a single perfect rosebud. With crimson velvet petals tightly furled, the promise of beauty was more exciting than the maturity of a full-blown rose. Alexandra was a woman who kept her word. The evocative scent wafted up to him, conjuring up visions of candlelight, wine, and a woman's soft lips.

Jake tried to act nonchalant and keep the grin from breaking out and betraying him. "Have we got anything to put this in?"

"I'll see." Janet walked to the door, put her hand on the door knob, turned.

"What does the card say?" She lifted an eyebrow. "Thank you for a lovely evening?"

He'd seen the card lying under the feathery greens. "No." Their pungent smell teasing his nose, he picked the card up, wondering if it might say something he shouldn't read aloud. Knowing Alexandra, he was sure it didn't. "It says, 'Thank you.'" At the knowing look in Janet's eyes, he added with exaggerated innocence, "That's all, I swear. Come and look at it yourself, if you don't believe me."

Her eyes said, *Buster, you must have done something to earn that rose,* but all her mouth said was, "I don't suppose there's a name."

Jake lifted his head. "As a matter of fact, there isn't."

If she'd worked for him longer and had known him better, Jake thought, she would have pressed him for more information. Instead, she went out of the door looking unsatisfied.

He'd never received flowers from a woman before. The rose carried no romantic or sexual connotations, coming as it did from Alex. It was, in effect, nothing more than a traditional way of saying thank you for spending time with her niece. But still, Jake found it oddly satisfying to know she'd made a special effort to bring him pleasure.

Should he call to tell her that it had arrived, and let her know how much he appreciated her thoughtfulness? Quickly, before he could change his mind, Jake reached for the phone.

He was put through to her immediately. "The rose is exactly what the doctor ordered," he said after her greeting.

"I'm glad. Does it have the right smell?"

"It has exactly the right smell." In the pause that followed, he realized suddenly that he was feeling self-conscious. "I'm planning to take Katherine out again on Sunday, if that's all right."

"That's fine." Alexandra's tone had a restraint he didn't like. The call wasn't going the way he wanted.

"Perhaps I'll see you then."

"If you do, it will be from behind a mound of work."

Alexandra said it kindly, but he got the message. He shouldn't expect his efforts with Katherine to change things between them.

Jake tried for a light, polite closing. "I'm sorry to hear it. Katherine and I will be thinking of you when we're out having fun."

"You do that," she said in that same impersonal, courteous voice.

When he'd said the perfunctory goodbye and hung up the phone, a succinct curse escaped his lips. When was he going to stop beating his head against a stone wall?

Maybe Katherine was right and he was wrong. Maybe it was stupid to keep trying with Alex. Maybe he had to face the truth. Alex didn't want anything to do with him. She wanted her life exactly as it was— without him in it.

Jake looked at the rose and felt his stomach muscles clench. He didn't like to give up, to admit failure. He didn't like to lose hope, whether it was for a seriously ill boy like Yosheko, or a blind, pigheaded woman like Alex.

But maybe it was time to admit the truth. Alex would never accept that part of his life where dreams were dashed into dust.

That was her prerogative. She had a right to decide how much pain she wanted in her life. She had a right to decide she didn't want him.

While he somehow—he had to learn to live without her.

Strange, how he'd never been able to learn that. In all the years they'd known each other, he realized abruptly, she'd always been there, in the back of his mind, a woman who was fun to tease, talk to, be with. She'd always been around, on holidays, at family gatherings. Now, because he'd wanted her to be his lover, he'd lost her as a friend. He wasn't sure which hurt the most.

He stared at the rose. It was beautiful, but in a few days it would wither and die. Maybe then, he'd find it easier to forget the woman who'd sent it to him.

Not bloody likely.

On Saturday morning, just before noon, there was a knock on Jake's condo door. He opened it to find a messenger with another long white box in his hand. He realized then that she meant to send him one every day for—what? Twelve days? Terrific. Twelve days of torture. Twelve more days of receiving flowers from a woman who didn't want him. The corners of his mouth lifted in a cynical smile. Just another of life's little ironies that fate seemed determined to serve up to him these days.

IT WAS A SUNDAY AFTERNOON and Alexandra had, as usual, brought work home. She'd spread everything out on the dining room table, but she couldn't concentrate on any of the purchase agreements that Sarah had compiled for her to study. The wind was blowing with gale force, rattling the window panes, whipping the palm trees, riling the ocean. Small craft warnings were up. The weather was freakish, the sun blazing from behind the clouds one moment, and hidden in a thick bank of clouds the next. She'd had to turn on the chandelier over the table to provide illumination when the sky went from blazing light to sudden darkness. There had been no rain as yet, but it was surely on its way.

"The wind just took off that pretty patio flag Helen bought the other day. There it goes out into the ocean. Aunt Alex?"

"Yes, dear?" Alexandra raised her head from her work to look at Katherine.

"Why do you suppose Jake hasn't called to tell me we aren't going sailing?"

That had bothered Alex, too. "I don't know. Maybe he just assumed we'd know."

"No. I don't think so. Jake wouldn't do that to me. He would have called me no matter what, or else come over anyway. Unless he couldn't. Unless something's wrong."

"I'll try calling him again." She'd rung his condo earlier, but there had been no answer. She'd called his office with the same results. His answering service said his associate was on duty that day and that they really didn't know where Dr. Hustead was. His mother was equally ignorant of his whereabouts.

Alexandra reached for the phone and dialed his number. She let it ring on and on, but there was no answer. Jake might be off duty, but he was rarely incommunicado.

"He's in trouble, I know he is."

Katherine's imaginative mind was beginning to make Alexandra's resonate with the same fear. Where on earth was the man?

"Couldn't you drive over to his condo? Maybe somebody there has seen him or knows where he went."

Alexandra flung down her pencil. "That's a good idea."

"Can I go with you?" Her eyes darkened. "Or should I stay here in case he calls?"

"Good thinking. You stay by the phone, I'll go check out his place."

ALEXANDRA PULLED UP in front of the two-story building that housed his condo, but when she stepped out of the car, some instinct made her walk around toward the back of the building where the rear entrance opened out onto the beach.

Against the gray of a roiling sea and sky, there was a dock of weathered wood extending into the ocean, and a boat bumping violently against it. On the other side of the dock, Jake strode across the sand into the water, lugging a Windsurfer with a huge pink sail. He was going out in the storm, with only a sailboard between him and the ocean.

Her heart leaped up and turned over. Was the man mad? She ran to stop him, her eyes fastened on Jake's naked back. He was dressed for surfing, his buttocks covered by a snug black swimsuit she'd never seen him wear before, his hair tousled by the wind, the turbulent water churning around his knees as he waded out into the wild sea. His shoulders had an odd tilt to them. His body was tense, strained, resolute. His only concession to safety was a small life belt wrapped around his waist. Hardly adequate protection in a gale like this.

"Jake!"

The wind choked her voice, muffled her words. She was so far away from him. She tried to run faster, but the sand gave under her sneakers, treacherously delaying her. The wind whipped her hair into streamers across her face. Time itself seemed to be holding her back, fastening her to the traitorous sand that wouldn't let her reach Jake.

He yanked the sail upright and stepped on the board. Before she could shake off her shock, he skimmed away from shore, his arms taut on the wishbone boom as he struggled to stay upright on a wind-maddened sea.

Why was he doing this? He wasn't an idiot. Jake was a sensible man who had a healthy respect for all human life, including his own. Right at the moment, though, he courted suicide with a reckless abandon that made Alexandra's heart rise in her throat. Jake had the look of a man who didn't give a damn about his life or anybody else's.

Out on the ocean, Jake clung to the boom with grim determination and struggled to stay upright, but a shift of the fierce wind slammed the sail into his shoulder and knocked him off the board. He went down cursing, water swamping his face, his eyes, his mouth. He spit and clung, scrambling to get back on the slippery, water-sleek board. The wind caught the sail and an ocean wave slapped him in the face. He slipped and went under again. He clung tenaciously, determined not to be bested. Using more care, he crawled onto the board, struggling to catch a breath, slammed his feet into the straps, then lurched upright. The sail flopped treacherously and the wind whipped his hair across his wet face obscuring his vision. He shook his head to free his vision and yanked up the sail, only to have the wind kick it out of his hands.

Jake went down on the board instantly, reaching into the water for the boom. He slipped and nearly fell headlong into the surf. He fought to regain his equilibrium, caught the boom and strained knees, thighs, biceps to bring up the sail. Bowing to the strength of his muscled body and his indomitable will, the sail jerked upright. The wind filled the cloth, and instantly, he was whizzing through the water at express train speed, his breath snatched from his lungs, the water lashing his cheeks.

He laughed harshly. This was what he needed. Violence. A battle that he could win. He would bend the elements to his will, the wind, the sea, the sail. He would not be defeated. He would win, even though it would be a shallow victory...

The sail twisted and he lost his balance, and fell into the sea.

WHEN JAKE WENT DOWN AGAIN, got up and headed out to sea at a breathtaking speed, Alexandra had had all she could take. She scanned the beach frantically. She saw a small aluminum fishing boat bumping beside the condo dock. Her feet made hollow sounds on the wood as she raced down the dock and jumped into the boat.

Would the motor start? If it did, would she reach him in time?

Alexandra pulled the cord and the motor choked and coughed. Frantic, she tried again. And again. She cursed, she prayed, she pulled on the rope—until at last the motor roared into life. She cast off the restraining rope and was immediately tossed sideways into the dock by the force of the wind and the water knocking against the freed bow. Gritting her teeth, she opened the throttle and headed out to sea where the pink sail was growing smaller on the horizon. Then the sky opened and it started to rain.

Jake had fallen again, Alexandra could tell by the way the pink sail was dragging on the water. And this time, he wasn't getting up.

She tried to get more power from the boat, but she already had the throttle open as far as it would go. Miles of ocean stretched between them, miles of churning waves, miles of treacherous water that could swallow a man in seconds.

Jake Hustead, if you drown, I'll never speak to you again. Hang onto that board....

So far away. Not getting any closer. Why can't I get any closer? *Jake. Don't die. You...can't...die....*

So long. Why is it taking so long? Why isn't the boat moving?

He's there. In the water. He's hanging onto the sailboard, but he's hurt. He's hit his head. He's bleeding.

She slowed the motor and circled. With the loss of power, the bow tossed and lifted with the wildness of the ocean. She had little or no control. Desperately, she scrambled over to the port side and reached for him, just as the wind took him out of her reach.

"Jake!"

He raised his head and looked at her, his eyes glazed, uncomprehending.

"Give me your hand."

He shook his head.

"Let go of the sailboard and give me your hand."

He shook his head again.

"Jake, let go!"

The sound of his name and her frantic scream penetrated his dazed consciousness. His hand opened, the sailboard drifted away. His other hand came up out of the water, too far away. Too frighteningly far away. But if she tried to get closer and missed him on this circuit, she might injure his legs with the turning blades of the idling motor.

She grabbed, missed, grabbed again and caught him. His fingers were chilled, wet, slippery. She tightened her grip on his hand and tried desperately to pull him into the boat, but he was heavy, so heavy. She needed more strength. She must have more strength. Crying, pleading, praying, she pulled and tugged. The boat rocked crazily and just as she thought they were tipping into the water, he was over the side and in, his legs in the air, his shoulders caught crazily between the boat seats. She pulled him around until he sat partially upright with his back against the seat. He was pale, the cut on his head bleeding profusely. But he was alive.

She wanted to hold him close, warm him, make sure he stayed conscious. But the wind screamed in her ears, the rain came down in a driving force, and the boat reared and bucked in the water. An urgent need to ensure their survival sent her scrambling to the back of the boat where she opened the throttle and headed for shore.

Alexandra nudged the boat up next to the dock and secured it, but she didn't bother trying the tricky maneuver of stepping onto the dock. She splashed out into the shallow water beside the boat and indicated for Jake to follow her. Now that the clawing fear had left her throat, it was easier to help him out of the boat, drape his arm over her shoulder and wade through the shallows with him.

At his back door, she halted, breathless. "Key under the flowerpot," he muttered.

She reached under the terra cotta pot, which held a yucca plant, and found his key. In seconds she had him inside his condo. They both stood dripping onto the beige rug. Jake looked too dazed to care. Nor did she. Her priority was getting him warm and dry and seeing to that cut.

"Which way is the bathroom?"

He gestured toward the hallway. Alexandra urged him forward, pushed him inside the small room, flopped the toilet seat down and pushed him onto it.

She snatched up a small blue towel lying on the counter, dampened it and began cleaning his head wound. Jake sat silent and stoic throughout her ministrations. In spite of the profuse bleeding the cut was small and superficial, she was relieved to see.

"Antiseptic?"

"My bag. Out by the door."

When she came back with his black doctor's bag and opened it, he showed her which bottle to use.

"Ouch!" he said when she applied the red liquid to his skin. "That stuff hurts."

"Don't like the taste of your own medicine, Doctor?" Alexandra was brusque and efficient, trying hard to control her trembling hands. The wound was bleeding again, and she was horrified by the thought that Jake might have knocked himself unconscious and drowned. She found a bandage and applied it with a little more force than was necessary, wishing the absurd urge she had to cry would go away.

"Do you have to be quite so efficient?" he grumbled.

"Yes." She turned to cap the bottle and return it to his bag, when he started to shiver. Alarmed, knowing chills were a sign of shock, she unbuckled the life belt he was wearing, dropped it to the floor and snatched a huge blue bath towel from the rack to wrap around his shoulders. He accepted it gratefully.

"Are you going into shock?"

"No. I'm just chilled from the air conditioning."

She stared down at his tousled head, the sight of him filling her with a dozen conflicting emotions. The fear was receding, but she could still taste it in her mouth, sharp, metallic. She could still feel the blood-numbing, all-consuming panic. Beyond the fear lurked a very strong urge to smack his bottom a good one.

"You'd beter get that wet suit off and get into a hot shower."

"You're wet, too." He clasped both her hips in his hands and steadied her while he dipped his head and laid his forehead against her abdomen with such stark need of her touch that every nerve in her body clenched. "Thank you for coming after me. You were very brave, but very foolish. I never meant to endanger you. You should have left me to drown. It would have been safer for you."

"What were you doing, just going out for a jolly spot of trying to kill yourself?"

"No. I just . . . wanted to fight something and win for a change."

She raised her hand, letting it hover over his head for a few minutes while she tried to resist the temptation to stroke him. Her fingers seemed to have a will of their own. She slid her hand over his hair like she would have done to a child, reveling in the feel of the wet, silky strands against her palm. "What battles have you been losing?"

Jake pushed away from her and dodged out from under her caressing hand. "Forget it. It doesn't concern you."

She gazed at him, sitting there on the toilet seat with a bandage on his head and a towel wrapped around his shoulders, trying to look self-contained and proud. The worst of it was, he succeeded. In two seconds, he'd distanced himself from her, and the hurt was sharper than she'd thought it could be.

"It's your young violin player, isn't it? Is he . . . worse?"

Jake's eyes slammed up to hers, as if she had hurt him. Alexandra reached out to ease the pain, catching his face in her hands. "Tell me. Please. I went out after you. I . . . have a right to know. I've got to know."

He twisted away from her touch and stared somewhere beyond her, shutting her out. She dropped her hands to her sides. How cold and empty they felt without the warmth of his cheeks between them. The ache inside her swelled, filling her with longing, need, and regret. She was getting exactly what she deserved. She'd told Jake she didn't want to share his life. He was only following her instructions.

How wrong she'd been to tell him that. She did want to share his life. She wanted to share it all, the joys, the hurts, everything.

The look on Jake's face told her it was too late. He didn't want her. Why should he? She'd made her feelings clear. She'd picked her road to travel by. A safe road. A poor lonely miserable road, but a safe one. And now she was stuck on it with no way to turn back.

Alexandra swung away from him and bowed her head. "You're right, of course. I don't have any rights where you're concerned—" She reached for the door knob.

"He's refused to go back into the hospital," Jake said in a cold, unemotional voice. "He says he can't take any more treatments. It's going to be a matter of weeks for him."

It hurt horribly to hear it stated so bluntly, so coldly. So hopelessly. She turned around to him, the sheen of tears in her eyes. "I'm sorry. So sorry..."

He gazed up at her with green glassy eyes filled with pain. "You were better off not knowing."

"No. Jake—"

His succinct epithet split the silence. Jake slung off the towel, stood up and turned around to strip off his swimsuit. His hand between his skin and the waistband, he turned back as if he'd just remembered she was there. "I don't blame you for not wanting the hassle. Why should you put up with the interrupted nights, the pain and the sorrow, for the somewhat dubious privilege of sharing my life?" His face was impassive. "You're a smart lady, Alex. Stay smart. Stay out of my life. Now if you'll excuse me, I'm going to take that shower."

Her eyes locked with his, she stood stock-still, waiting. The wall had gone up, stronger and higher than before. Could she breach it again?

Jake made an impatient gesture with his hand. "You did your good deed for the day, you rescued the idiot doctor from the storm-tossed sea. You're all done now. There's nothing more for you to do. I'll be fine."

Alexandra's damp clothing and her emotional need for Jake sent chills skimming over her arms.

His eyes roved over her wet, clinging T-shirt. Not a muscle moved in his face. "Get out, Alex. Now. Before I forget all the fine, noble sentiments I just expressed and take what you're offering."

She shook her head, an unreasonable hope clogging her throat.

"Alex—" He sounded grim, cold, hostile.

It took all her courage to hold her ground. "I want to stay with you."

His mouth twisted in a cynical grimace. "Feeling sorry for me, are you? Do us both a favor and control your sympathetic urges."

Alexandra clung tenaciously to the remnants of her pride. "I want to be with you. In every way there is." She lifted her chin, her silvery-blue eyes dark. "If...you still want me."

"I don't want you—" at the look on her face, he growled "—not like this. Not caught up in...an idiotic emotional backlash that will make you hate yourself—and me—in the morning."

"I'll never hate you, Jake. I never have and I never will. Please let me...stay with you."

Alexandra hadn't known she would ever beg. But she was begging. Begging with her eyes, with her body, with her mouth. She seemed to have lost all her pride. "Please. Please let me just . . . hold you."

Jake's eyes darkened with a sudden flare of heat that sent her spirit soaring. "I want more than holding from you."

"Then. . . let me give you what you want." She raised her head and she looked as proud as he. "What we both want."

"It would be much better for you if we didn't . . . get involved."

A token protest at best. His voice had softened and so had his face.

Alexandra tried to keep her soaring spirits under control and match Jake's soberness. "You're right, of course. It would be better for . . . both of us. There's so much at stake, our professional lives, our friendship—" a tiny smile crept over her lips "—our sanity."

He was fighting not to smile back. A wellspring of emotion bubbled up within her. She knew as well as he did that while every word was coolly sensible, the atmosphere had changed.

Alexandra felt her chest moving in shallow, quick breaths. Jake stood still, waiting, watching, handing the responsibility for whatever happened entirely to her.

She swallowed and stepped up to him, reaching for the waistband of his swim briefs to draw them down his hips. He caught her hands and brought them roughly up to his chest. "Are you sure you know what you're doing?"

In the intense silence, Alexandra's eyes searched Jake's and found what they were looking for. Need. A need as desperate as her own. "Yes, I'm sure." She slipped her hands out from under his and tried for a lighter tone. "I'm undressing you. Unless . . . you object."

He gazed down into her face so intently that it seemed to Alexandra he was physically touching her nose, her cheeks, the strand of hair clinging to her forehead. Then he smiled that wonderful, half-mocking smile. "Do you see me objecting?"

Encouraged, she slid her hands around his back, under the waistband, cupping her palms over his bare buttocks.

"You don't waste any time, do you?" He brushed her lips with his mouth in a teasing kiss. A kiss of acceptance.

When he raised his head, the erotic promise in Jake's eyes seared her with delight. "Efficient use of time is the first thing a good executive learns," she said with a knowing look.

"I never thought I'd be grateful for your business school education." He sounded more than grateful. He sounded profoundly aroused, his voice husky with passion.

Alexandra drew his suit down over his rear, past his thighs, his knees, his calves. When she had the swim briefs down to his ankles, he lifted one foot and then the other, freeing himself.

She straightened, drinking in the sight of him, the lean strength of his body, the aroused glory of his manhood. Her heart pounding with excitement and the thrill of knowing she could affect him so quickly and so thoroughly, she averted her eyes from his all-too potent male allure, grasped the bottom of her T-shirt and asked politely, "Help me off with this, will you?"

He shook his head slowly. "Uh-uh. I'd rather watch." He waited, a sensual smile teasing his lips upward.

Her long, dark lashes flickering down over her eyes, she lifted her arms, pulled her shirt up over her head, tossed it aside.

Jake stood still, but he looked visibly moved at the sight of her vulnerable throat, the smooth roundness of her breasts encased in the bits of peach lace and silk. When she didn't move, Jake said softly, "Very becoming." His smile broadened into an audacious grin. "I'd rather see it going."

Her hair fell over her cheek as she leaned forward to unhook her bra. She was no longer cold. Her skin was hot, her body filled with a wild excitement, a feeling of walking too close to the rim of a chasm. This was love play with an edge. A tingling urgency spiraled up, making her loins sting with expectancy. The clasp gave. Avoiding his eyes, she slid one strap from her shoulder and then the other. The bra fell to the floor.

His face taut, Jake stepped toward her and inserted his fingers into the sides of her briefs. "You helped me with mine, I'll help you with these. It's only. . . fair."

It wasn't fair at all to feel the enchantment of his hands cupping her bare hips, promising further delights from those sensitive fingertips. Her breath stopped in her throat while her heart raced, sending suddenly heated blood through her body. Slowly, he bent, taking her last garment with him, his long, clever fingers cool as they glided down her legs, making a fire rise under her skin. Carefully, he locked his hands around her ankles, shackling her. Alexandra looked down at his darkly tousled head, his touch filling her with an odd mixture of passion and tenderness. He lifted her feet as she had for him, freeing her of her last scrap of clothing.

When Jake straightened, every nerve in Alexandra's body sang with anticipation. His eyes sought hers, drank from them before his gaze wandered lower to absorb the beauty of her naked body.

He reached out and touched the tip of her breast with one questing finger. She quivered with desire. He seemed not to notice, but his smile deepened.

"So very... feminine, so... mysterious. So... ripe and complete. I saw you, you know. The night you swam nude in the ocean. I felt as if I was seeing into the heart of you." He paused, his face darkly eloquent. "Now I feel as if you've given me your soul."

In a blaze of love, Alexandra reached for Jake, clasping him around the waist, clinging to him for support while his words and touch wreaked havoc through her, her back arched to allow him access to the place he sought.

"I didn't know you were there, that night," she whispered. "If I had, I would have come to you."

"Would you?" A husky request for assurance.

"Yes. I've been wanting this for a long time..."

"Not as long as I have, love," Jake said with a velvety soft intensity. "I seem to have been wanting you since the day I was born."

His thighs were hard and muscular against hers. She leaned back like a dancer, thrusting her hips into the cradle of his while she freed her upper body for his touch.

Jake took her breast fully into his hand, his palm covering it. Heat enveloped her. His eyes were bottomless depths of ocean green, consuming her.

She stroked up his back. "Darling, you're so cold. You've got to get under the shower—"

"Warm me. Now."

"Jake, I—" She was going to ask him if he wouldn't be more comfortable in bed. The look in his eyes stopped her words in her throat. He wasn't thinking about being comfortable. He was thinking about easing his killing thirst for her.

Silently, he asked the question. Her answer was a soft sigh, a caress on his hair. He groaned and lifted her up, letting her slide down his belly. He held her there, suspended between denial and possession. Waiting.

All womanly enticement, Alexandra leaned forward and sought his mouth with hers, letting her kiss tell him how much she wanted him.

When she raised her head, he murmured her name in an agony of relief, and, as easily as if they'd done it a million times before, he slipped his male hardness into her warm sheath in the oldest dance of all.

Rapture spiraled upward in light waves, rippling through Alexandra, making her shudder with pleasure. She looked down into his eyes and saw that Jake was as shattered as she by the shimmering, fiery pleasure of their joining.

"Easy," he murmured in a soft, dark voice, "easy, my love."

His hands slipped under her buttocks, holding her. She gripped his shoulders and wrapped her legs around his hips, lost in the wonder, the ease, the rightness of his body filling hers.

Nothing in her life had ever been like this, nothing. The excitement, the ecstasy brought her a wild, joyful aliveness.

All because of Jake. Only he would dare to take her with such self-assured, arrogant novelty. Only he could push her to the edge of the cliff and keep her hanging there so subtly, love her so completely. And only he could gaze into her eyes and take his pleasure from watching her gasp with delight.

Alexandra dug her fingers into his shoulders, asking for more, asking for completeness.

"Wait, love. Wait just a little longer—"

She wanted to do as he asked, cling to the fire and make it last. But he was thrusting deep and slow and true, making her cry out for more, and more . . .

Jake. Jake was the power and the rapture, the driving force she needed to breathe, to live. And she was the vessel, accepting his strength and giving it back to him tenfold.

He muttered her name in that guttural sound of tortured pleasure, praising her for her courage, her beauty, her wildness. She arched back in an agony of delight. He kissed her throat, her breasts, and whispered how wonderful she was and how good she made him feel. He dazzled her with the sensuality of his words, his body, his eyes. He was totally hers, every cell in his being dedicated to her pleasure.

His words, the sultry eroticism in his eyes, the feel of his skin rubbing against hers, the fullness of him inside her, made it impossible for her to contain the ecstasy any longer. It gathered and peaked, shattering her.

Alexandra cried Jake's name. He tightened his hold on her hips and thrust into her wild, consuming rhythm. She clung to him, riding out the storm. He threw his head back and groaned, his throat taut with the pleasure shuddering through his body.

"I'M TOO HEAVY FOR YOU." Alexandra moved slightly, asking for release.

Jake smiled. "You don't hear me complaining, do you?"

"You were never much for complaining."

"That's me," he said softly, teasingly, circling his hips against hers, "Bearing hardship with grace and valor, stoic to the end. And what a lovely little end it is." He tightened his hold on her buttocks, shifting her slightly, but keeping her exactly where she was, even though she could feel his body withdrawing from hers.

"You idiot. Put me down before you break your back."

"I don't think I will." His face was dark with possession. "I'd rather keep you here. Something might come up again that I need you to . . . attend to."

She laughed at him, but a slow, sultry heat curled inside her at the thought he wanted to make love to her again so soon. "Put me down before you hurt yourself. How would we explain what happened to the emergency room doctor?"

"Carter would eat his heart out with envy." As if he was satisfied he'd teased her long enough, he loosened his hold on her hips and let her feet slide to the floor. She was still languid from their lovemaking, every nerve relaxed, her knees weak.

Her body seemed to have forgotten how to stand. Alexandra grasped his shoulders for support. "And think about all the adoring women you'd have hovering around you. How would you explain your ailment to your mother, my mother and Katherine—*Katherine!* She was worried out of her mind about you. I've got to call her."

With Jake's eyes claiming possession of her and that maddeningly wonderful smile tugging at the corners of his mouth, she snatched a towel off the towel rack and immediately became all thumbs when she tried to wrap it around herself.

Gently, he pushed her hands away with his deft doctor's touch, pulled the towel over her breasts and tucked the end neatly and solidly under. He stepped back to survey his handiwork and was pleased to see she was flushed with bemusement and lingering arousal. "She can't see you through the phone, love."

She laid her hand along the side of his throat with a tenderness that turned his insides to melted butter. "It was nice of you to help me with the towel first and then point out I didn't need it."

"I'm a nice guy," he murmured.

Her smile turned a little wicked. "Good, yes. Nice, I doubt." She turned her back to him and neatly dodged the swat he tried to give her as she headed for the bedroom phone.

Jake found himself following her. Wandering after her like a lost puppy was just one more sign that he was besotted and unable to let her out of his sight, but he didn't care. He leaned against the doorjamb, watching her bend over to dial the phone, her other hand clutching at the towel.

Katherine must have picked up the phone on the first ring. Alexandra made conciliatory noises into the receiver Jake didn't catch. Then she said, "Jake is fine, sweetheart, really. And so am I."

To Alexandra, the anxiety Katherine tried so hard to hide came through the phone loudly and clearly. To a girl who'd lost her parents in a thunderstorm, the short span of time since Alex had arrived at Jake's condo must have seemed like a year. Feeling guilty, she clutched at the slipping towel. "Yes, I'm fine, too." As if the force of Jake's thoughts drew her, she turned and looked at him. His eyes mocked her, telling her she was more than fine. "How about you?" Alexandra said into the phone. "The wind didn't do anything to the house, did it? Is Grandma okay?"

In the same stilted voice, Katherine assured Alexandra that her grandmother, the house and she had weathered the storm. "How soon are you coming home?"

Once more she turned to Jake. Dark, lean, naked, he made her think dark naked thoughts, thoughts of wanting to stay with him forever and of never having to leave his bedroom—or his life. "I don't know just when I'll be back—"

"Tell her you're going to have dinner first," Jake commanded softly from the doorway.

Alexandra hesitated. Then, as Jake's eyes roved over her face, asking, seeking, caressing, she said into the phone, "I'll be home right after we eat."

With two more assurances that she would be home as soon as she could, Alexandra eased Katherine's fears and gently said goodbye to her.

She turned and faced him across the softly lit bedroom. "She was worried about you."

"She didn't know I was in such good hands."

Incredibly, he was aroused again. Beautifully aroused. Looking at him made currents flow deep within her and hungers rise up demanding to be fed. "Jake, I—"

"Are you going shy on me?"

She shook her head, unable to answer, her eyes locked with his.

"Shall we try it in bed this time, like conventional people?"

Suddenly, he was in front of her, his lean tanned hand with its dusting of sun-bleached hair reaching for the top of her towel he'd so carefully tucked in only a few minutes ago.

"This time there's no heat-of-the-moment, no pretending it's all in the name of first aid," he said softly, bringing her eyes winging up to him in shocked surprise. Slowly, he drew her towel away as if he were unwrapping the finest of diamonds. His eyes drifted over her body, making her feel as if she'd been touched by a fall of cobwebby lace. "This is sheer, delightful going to bed together. I think this is how it all starts."

His eyes fastened on hers, he reached out and cupped a breast gently in his hand, fingering the nipple that was already tight with anticipation.

"Are you sure?" she whispered. "It doesn't feel like a beginning."

"What does it feel like, love?" he said, his gaze dark and hungry on her face.

"It feels like we're somewhere in the middle. And it started long before, so long ago I can't remember precisely when."

His gentle but insistent hands pushed her down on the bed with a touch that was like thistledown on her shoulders. The merest whisper of possession. She nestled back against the pillows. He came down over her, his weight on his hands. The skin of his shoulders was taut and dark, his hair falling forward on his brow, his body sheened in the light. She stared up into his green eyes, those deeply intense, hungry eyes, and it seemed so impossible that look was meant for her alone. Impossible . . . and utterly right.

Her spirit soared. This was what it was to feel . . . alive. She raised her hand to touch his cheekbone, the whorl of his ear, the tip of his nose. Hers. This hard-boned elegant face that she knew as well as her own, this mouth that had taunted and teased her more times than she cared to remember, this beautiful dark head with its complex combination of ideas, thoughts, hopes, dreams, was, for a little while at least, hers.

He groaned and pressed his face into her neck. She could feel him shudder with strong emotion. When he lifted his head, his eyes were glossy. "It's a rough river we're starting down, love. But we're in it now. And there's no turning back . . ."

She wasn't sure what he was talking about. But when he dropped his head to her breasts and with his tongue and lips made her feel like the most beautiful woman in the world, then explored her navel and finally, inevitably, wandered to the mound of curls below, she forgot that there was anything about him she didn't understand. For he seemed to understand everything about her. "Jake, please—"

"Not yet, love," he murmured against her skin.

She was on fire, burning, wanting the pleasure, yet holding back. He gave and gave until suddenly, he moved over her and she was able to take him deep within her and feel him move with a freedom that made her senses reel.

"No," he said, when she turned away in that exquisite agony of pleasure. "No." He captured her face and turned it toward his. "I want to watch you. I want to look at you . . . and have you look at me while I . . ." He arched his back in a groan of pleasure, every muscle in his neck taut, and watching him, the stinging jolt of pure pleasure burned through her, making them one in their ecstasy.

LAZILY, HE SLID a caressing hand down her cheek and wrapped his fingers around her shoulder. "What about that shower? I'd like to take it now . . . with you." His tone of voice held the teasing sweetness of a sated lover.

"You mean I don't have to leave to protect your modesty like you wanted me to do before?" Her drawl was as teasing as his.

"You leave now and you take your life in your hands."

"I haven't already?"

His eyes caught hers, darkened. "No." He took her palms, brought them up to his mouth and placed a kiss in one, then the other. "I intend to take very good care of you."

Alexandra raised a hand to slide it along his throat, his jaw. She felt languid and wanton, secure in her sensuality. "I didn't know it could be like this."

He smiled, the lift of his mouth male, arrogant, self-assured. "I'll take that as a compliment."

"You would."

"About that shower . . ."

"Are you looking for repression, or rejuvenation? In other words, is the water going to be hot or cold?"

He tugged at her hand to lift her up, she resisted him. "Why don't you just come along peacefully and find out?"

He took hold of her wrists with a very businesslike grip and brought her to her feet.

"Tenacious man, aren't you?" she said as he brought her up into his arms. Only now, after her need for him had been satiated, did she feel the sweet harmony of their bodies, the way she fit him like a glove.

"Only when I'm dealing with truculent women."

"I've never been truculent in my life. But I have a feeling I could learn to be if I hang around you long enough—"

She snuggled against him, savoring the feel of her breasts nuzzled against his chest, her lips cradled in his.

He raised a dark eyebrow and gave her a mocking look. "Somehow I don't think truculence is what you're learning."

"No?" she asked with a smile, as sweet as a fallen angel's.

He shook his head. "I have a feeling we'd better take that shower soon, or we're going to end up right back in that bed."

"Bragging or complaining?"

"You are a saucy wench, aren't you? I've never seen this side of you before."

"I've never had this side of me before. Not until you." She said it with all her heart, sincerity shining from her eyes.

His gaze darkened and he leaned down and kissed her. Then, he swept her up and carried her into the bathroom, depositing her on the soft fluffy rug in front of the tub. Looking as though he hated to be separated from her for even a second, he stepped to the shower to turn on the water. His back was to her and his nicely muscled buttocks were too much a temptation. Alexandra remembered how she'd wanted to spank him for endangering his life on that wild and windy ocean, and gave one cheek a light tap.

Jake swung around, his eyes bright with a feigned threat. "You are full of surprises, aren't you? You do that again, lady, and you *will* be taking your life in your hands."

So of course, she had to try it again. And of course, he had to pull her under the shower, trap her in the corner and kiss her senseless in retribution. Then, as her body softened against his and her wet breasts pressed against his hairy chest, the water streamed over them, and there was no retribution, only the wild joy of desire flaring out of control once again, and silken skin fitting inside silken skin.

8

IN THE GATHERING DARKNESS of the early evening, Jake lay in bed with his arm around Alexandra. While she dozed, he stared down at her in the soft gray light, a frown drawing his brows together. She slept with her head tucked into his shoulder and her breasts nudging his chest. He looked at her, his gaze wandering over her soft throat, her lashes a dark shadow against her cheek, the soft ripeness of her mouth made swollen by his kisses. Wrapped in a cocoon of quiet beside her, he felt as fiercely protective toward her as a father with his child.

Jake hadn't known it was possible to feel this way. For centuries men must have felt protective toward their women as they lay by their side in the aftermath of love, but to Jake, it was more than a little frightening.

Alexandra didn't want him to feel protective. Nor did she want him to feel possessive. She was an independent woman with an established life-style and a career of her own. She didn't want him encroaching on her life. She'd told him so repeatedly.

Only a little while ago, however, he'd encroached on her life quite thoroughly.

He wondered what she really felt about him and about their being together? He wondered if, when she opened those wonderful blue eyes of hers, she'd look at him with love or contempt.

Maybe he deserved her contempt. He'd wanted her and he'd taken her. It seemed as though he'd been wanting her for days, months, years. And when she'd made it clear that she wanted him too, he'd taken advantage of her sympathy for him and obliged her. Quickly—before she could change her mind.

Now, as the storm died away and the far-off rumblings of thunder grew fainter and fainter, he had time to think about what he'd done. He hadn't acted responsibly. He hadn't asked her if she was protected, nor had he tried to protect her. Hell of a doctor he was. Put Alex within three feet of him and he forgot everything and acted like a seventeen-year-old kid high on hormones. He'd have to ask her if she was protected.

Alexandra moved slightly and turned toward him, her breasts brushing his chest. Now his body knew exactly what pleasure awaited him when it was joined with hers, and his nerves leaped to life at her slightest touch. The tickle of her hair against his shoulder set his nerves humming. Her slender fingers brushed his thigh, and his loins reacted with a hot clenching.

So much for good intentions. He was awake and alive and wanting her again, and he had a feeling it would be a long, long time before his hunger for her would ever be completely satisfied.

He pulled away a little, freeing her pink nipple from where it had nestled in his chest hairs. He'd hoped to ease the heat within him, but instead he created a deeper need for the feel of her. A need he had to fill.

Taut with anticipation, he brought his hand up from her thigh. As if he were gathering thistledown, he cupped her breast. The weight of it resting in his palm filled him with satisfaction, even while the restless stirring in his gut awakened a deep, needy hunger all over again.

She made a soft sound of pleasure and lifted a hand to his neck. Her eyes were still closed. "Umm, that feels good."

It was incredibly intimate to lie with Jake like this, letting him look and touch at his leisure. It was easier to keep her eyes closed, easier to pretend she wasn't an eager participant. But if he kept on touching her with such tenderness, her participation would be inevitable.

"You're awake," he said. But he didn't move his hand.

"Sort of. Half."

More than half-awake, Jake thought, a sensual smile curling his lips. He could see from the awareness in her body that she was starting to get aroused again. The sleepy relaxed ease of her body was changing into something more—aware. She lay very still, a tautness in her shoulders, hips and thighs that told him she was enjoying his lazy caressing.

"Did you get enough sleep?" He circled the rosy tip of her breast with a curious finger and watched it harden, deeply satisfied with his ability to arouse her.

"Enough sleep for . . . what?"

He gave up all pretense of casualness and leaned over her, his green eyes looking deeply into hers. "Enough to talk about something we should have talked about before we made love."

Her eyes flashed over his face, reading in it his concern for her. He gazed into her eyes. Silvery-blue, as deep and dark as the ocean. He wanted to drown in them. "It's . . . all right, Jake."

He studied her expression intently, searching for signs of shyness or prevarication. "Are you sure?"

She nodded, not wanting to admit that she'd known deep in her heart it was only a matter of time before she became his lover, and she'd made her own preparations.

"Don't fob me off with that old *it's the wrong time of the month* line, Alex."

"I'm not. I've been . . . taking precautions."

He propped himself up on his elbow and stared down into her face. "You knew this would happen." He smiled at her, a dark, sensual, pleased smile.

She moved her hand up to slide it along his jaw, his cheek. "No, I didn't know this would happen. But I hoped." Her wandering fingertip investigated his cheek, his nose, his wonderful full mouth.

He looked as dark and pleased as a pasha as he took her hand and brought it to his mouth to press a kiss in her palm, then flick the sensitive skin with the tip of his tongue.

She lifted her eyes to his. "I care about you, Jake. I care . . . desperately. It's just that I can't . . . I've always wanted too much. I'm all wrong for you—"

His expression stayed smooth and dark and undisturbed, even while he eased his body on top of hers, finding the fit of their hips. "Let's not think about the ways you're wrong for me. Let's think about the ways you're right for me—" he said, enjoying her response as she lifted her hips to meet his, joining their bodies in a hungry need that matched his own "—so right. Oh, my love, so very right."

"THE PHONE IS RINGING," Alexandra said.

The room was dark. He switched on a small lamp by

his side of the bed and after a quick, frowning glance at her, reached for the receiver.

It was over. Their interlude was over, as she'd known it would be. The phone was reaching out to Jake, calling him back . . .

He said hello, listened. Then, with a face dark with satisfaction, he thrust the receiver down into the soft pillows next to her ear. "It's for you."

Her eyes darkened with surprise. Jake looked like he'd been given a Christmas present, his mouth curved in a sensual, pleased smile. Thoroughly enjoying himself, supremely confident in his nakedness, Jake hitched back to lean against the headboard, one leg casually bent at the knee in the nest of rumpled sheets. Rattled by receiving a telephone call at his house and being exposed to the full force of his male beauty, Alexandra took the phone from his hand. Jake looked as self-satisfied as a sheikh fresh from his woman's bed, and he smiled with the same dark beauty. She did her best to look unmoved, but his tanned, hairy body and natural grace gave him the sexual punch of a male perfume advertisement. She fought for self-control. "Who is it?"

"Katherine."

"Katherine?" Alexandra clutched the sheet to her breasts and sat up. Into the phone she said, "Sweetheart, what's wrong?"

"I thought you would be home by now." The girl sounded cool, hurt. "I wanted to call you earlier, but Grandma said no."

"I'll be home just as I promised . . . right after we eat."

"You haven't eaten dinner yet? It's almost nine o'clock. What have you and Jake been doing all this time?"

Alexandra's eyes flashed up to Jake's. His broad wonderfully bare chest, one hand idly playing with a strand of her hair, he smiled at her with a knowing look. "Go ahead, love," he murmured, "tell her what you've been doing all this time."

Alexandra dragged her eyes away from his nude beauty, thinking she might—just might—be able to put two thoughts together and salvage this telephone conversation if she stopped looking at him. "I . . . we've been . . . talking." Quickly before Katherine could say more, she added, "I'll . . . be home soon, I promise."

When she was satisfied that Katherine believed her, she said goodbye to her niece and handed the phone to Jake. He replaced it carefully and returned her gaze, all innocence.

"You devil. You loved that, didn't you?"

Arms folded over his chest, Jake thought about it. "I enjoy watching you prevaricate. You do it so badly."

Alexandra leaned against the headboard of the bed and glared with mock ferocity at her teasing lover, her body alive with the stirring hunger she thought he'd appeased with his lavish ministrations.

He knew her too well. One glance and Jake accurately assessed the awakening of desire in her face and body. Not a man to waste an opportunity, he leaned over her and compounded her disturbed state by murmuring, "Let's . . . talk . . . some more." His insistent fingers tugged at the sheet she held.

"I can't, Jake."

Unperturbed, he stretched down and kissed her bare shoulder. "One telephone call and you're ready to run away?" The words were soft and light, but their meaning was clear. He'd been called away during another storm when they'd nearly made love and because of the interruption, she'd tried to put him out of her life. What was she going to do now that she'd been caught in the same situation? He went on speaking in the same light tone that carried a thousand undercurrents. "Katherine isn't a baby. And Beatrice is there with her."

"I don't want her to know that I—"

"—have the normal needs of a mature woman? Or that I'm your lover?"

"Jake, I can't deny what happened."

His eyes darkened dangerously. "Oh, yes, you can. You're already denying it."

Her eyes locked with his, their dark blue depths heated. "What do you want from me?"

"Just a simple admission of the facts. We made love, and we will again." After a brief pause, he continued. "Because it's what we both want."

She shook her head and threw the sheet back. He lunged across the bed and pulled her back into the pillows with the weight of his chest, his hands on her wrists. Instantly, he eased his weight away and kept her prisoner by the hold he had on her arms. "You're not leaving my bed until *you* say it, too."

She lay there, the sheet that had been covering her gone, looking wanton, feeling wanton, knowing her nakedness was laid out like a feast for him to see, that her hair lay in tangled confusion around her shoulders, that her eyes were dark with the sensual arousal his naked, possessive maleness was already arousing again. She wriggled against the softness of the pillows in a futile attempt to escape, but his grip on her was unyielding. She went utterly still and stared up at him, trying mightily to be annoyed with him, intensely aware of the smile that threatened to soften her resolve.

"I don't like your caveman techniques."

He took a long time letting his eyes wander over her, taking in the darkness of her eyes, the flush at her throat. "Yes, you do," he drawled at last. "You like everything about me. You told me so."

"I didn't—"

"Not with your mouth. With your eyes."

He leaned over and rewarded first one, and then the other, with two of the lightest and sweetest of butterfly kisses she'd ever known.

She might have had a chance fighting his self-assurance, but his tenderness left her defenseless. Alexandra reached up, clasped his head, pulled him down to her and kissed him fiercely on the mouth, the sweetness of the intimacy they'd already shared and her growing hunger for him coalescing into one searing kiss.

When he lifted his head, his smile was beautiful to behold. "That was a vote of confidence, I hope?" His eyes glittered with a pleased expectancy.

"What else do you want?"

"I want you to say, 'Jake is my lover.'" This was a game from their childhood, one they'd often played, his demanding she say what he decreed. But they'd never played it like this, with his hand dropping to her breast and teasingly tracing the areola, promising heaven, delivering small, anticipatory thrills in a game meant for adults only.

Her eyes met his. "You're being ridiculous—"

"Say it, Alex."

She lay unmoving, aware of his hand on her breast, the flick of his dark emerald eyes, the sensual curve of his mouth. He was on that delicious edge between complete satisfaction and a new excursion into seduction. Alexandra knew her slightest look or nod of agreement would send them into another round of lovemaking that would last another hour...or all night. She must resist him, she had to resist him. Yet, his hair was mussed because she had mussed it, glorying in the freedom to touch and tousle, and his throat was warm because she'd feathered kisses over it. What right did she have to deny him this one last intimacy? And even if she wanted to, could she? He might pretend to be playing with her, but under the playfulness was the rock hard determination she knew so well.

Alexandra lifted her hand to his cheek, feeling the coarse bristles of his night beard under her palm— masculine—hers. "You were...wonderful." She paused. The watchful waiting in his eyes told her he liked her praise, but he wanted exactly what he'd asked for and no less. She swallowed. "You made me proud to be a woman. I haven't felt like that for a long, long time. You're my lover, Jake...and I'm very glad."

He breathed in sharply, a deep flush of pleasure coming up over his throat. Her words had moved him, shaken him. He pulled her to him, his mouth coming down on hers, his tongue taking her with a passionate tenderness that moved her to the depths of her being. He had been inside her, yet this was more intimate.

She'd given him her vulnerability and he was giving it back a thousand times over. She'd admitted his power over her and he, in an act of consummate generosity, had given it back tenfold.

She was consumed with love. She burned to meet his generosity with a gift of her own. She moved, pulling him over her. Surprised, not fully aware of her intention, he lifted himself slightly to ease the weight of his body on hers. Filled with elation and an ancient, erotic female power, she surged upward and filled her feminine sheath with him.

He groaned, first with shock and then with ecstasy. She moved with him, loving him, loving him. He accepted her erotic commands willingly, eagerly. She slid her hands down his back and clutched his buttocks, pulling him closer, closer. He murmured to her to go slowly. She ignored him and went on plying him with the sweetness and sensual delights she seemed to have learned only from him, until the beauty and the brilliance were too much for either of them to bear.

When at last he pulled away from her and took a deep breath, his smile sparkled with satiety. "Love, when you surrender, you do it with style."

Jake's smiles were contagious. She smiled back at him, her mouth curving with the new self-confidence in her sensuality that Jake had given her. "Now, Og from the clan of the cavemen, if you're satisfied, would you mind letting me up?"

"I mind it very much. I'd rather keep you right where you are. But if you insist . . ."

He rolled away from her, went to the closet, pulled out a warm terry robe in pristine white that looked as if he'd never worn it and tossed it to her. While she put it on, he pulled another one from his closet for himself, one that was older, thinner, and a dark shade of navy blue toweling. When he'd tied the belt into a knot around his waist, he took her hand and tugged her into the kitchen, giving her a little shove toward the stove. "Do your thing, woman."

She spun around, compliance gone. "Now wait a minute. This is where I draw the line at the caveman act."

He stared at her, all feigned surprise.

"Jake, you know I don't cook."

"Not even scrambled eggs?"

"Not since I was thirteen." She cast him a saucy look. "I thought you were the expert in the kitchen, Cornish game hens and all that."

His eyes skimmed away from hers. "That's when I'm doing my best to keep my associate happy, and I have hours to shop and prepare. Impromptu meals aren't my style. Don't worry about it. We'll find something."

A search of Jake's cupboards for snacks netted them a can of olives, a can of cocktail shrimp, and a jar of cashews. Jake sat down on the corner of the table and stretched out his leg to rest his foot on the edge of Alexandra's chair. He wanted to watch her eat, he said. She would have protested, but he had challenge written all over his face. Filled with a need to meet that challenge, she handed him the olives and took the fork he gave her for the shrimp.

"You're big on hors d'oeuvres, I see."

He grinned. "Never know when folks might stop by, and of course I'd want to make them feel welcome." He picked up a cashew and popped it into her mouth, leaning back a little to watch her chew.

"Yes, I can see how a nice case of upset stomach would make them feel right at home. You wouldn't by any chance be drumming up business, would you, Doctor?"

He drew back in exaggerated shock. "Me? Never." Settling in comfortably on top of the table, he opened a bottle of wine and poured out a glass for her. It was blush wine, as pink as cotton candy, dry, and very good. They clinked glasses, their eyes toasting each other.

They'd consumed nearly half of the cocktail shrimp when Jake stabbed his fork into one Alexandra had aimed for. Her fork tangled with his. "On guard," Jake yelled, jumping down off the table and taking the stance of a fencing master.

"On guard yourself," Alexandra cried, and the battle of the forks was joined. They circled, brows furrowed with concentration, forks at the ready. He lunged, she dodged. Steel clashed on steel. Alexandra caught his fork tines in hers and was tasting premature triumph when, with one flip of his wrist, Jake sent her fork flying.

"Not fair," she cried, instinctively stepping back, now that she was unarmed. "You've had all that practice wielding hypodermic needles."

Jake stretched to his full height, pointed the fork at her midriff and started toward her, his mouth twisted in a wicked pirate's grin. "Now I'll get you, my pretty."

He backed her into the corner of the counter. His hands encircled her neck, but they were tender, not punishing. She offered him no resistance. Instead, she lifted her mouth hungrily to his. He tensed with a hunger that matched hers, slid his hands down her back to her hips and brought them up to fit into the cradle of his. Then, he bent his head and took her generous, sweet and swollen mouth.

His kiss was warm, rich with welcoming tenderness, fun, and the intimacies they'd shared. When at last he dragged his mouth away from hers and pressed her head into his chest, she sighed. "I have to go, Jake."

Three points of a metal fork pressed into the small of her back. Above her head he growled like a back street gangster, "You ain't goin' nowhere, baby."

She leaned back and gazed up at him, wishing she had half his sense of fun, a tenth of his uninhibited good nature, a hundredth part of his courage. She loved everything about him—his humor, his élan, his unreserved giving and accepting of sexual pleasure. She loved him.

Jake took one look at her face, tossed the fork onto the table and buried his mouth in her hair. "Damn. How am I supposed to let you go when you look at me like that?"

How could it feel so good to have his mouth travel over the softness of her cheek, over skin that remembered his mouth so well and wanted more? But Alexandra couldn't take what she wanted. The real world waited.

Jake was her lover now, sensitive to every nuance of her supple body. He easily detected her subtle withdrawal for what it was, a request for release. He let her put a little distance between them and looked down into her face, watching her mouth curve upward in amusement. "Some lover I must be. Why are you smiling, love?"

"I was wondering what I'm going to tell Katherine and my mother I had for dinner."

"Me," he murmured. "Tell them you had me."

"And very tasty you were, too." She pushed gently at him. "Really, Jake, I have to go."

"No." The word was warm, redolent of sexual promise.

"Yes." She was cool, honest, sincere.

"Stay the night with me."

"I can't—"

"Dammit, Alex, you're a grown woman. What difference does it make if Katherine, your mother, the whole damned world knows you're sleeping with me?"

"It makes a difference to me. I can't—I'm not ready to face all the problems our being publicly... committed to each other may bring. Not just yet. I need... time."

He released her instantly. "Of course." He stepped back, courteous, distant. Separate. No longer hers.

She wanted to go to him, to hug him and tell him everything would be all right, and to have him assure her as well. But she couldn't. There were questions in his brilliant green eyes she couldn't answer. Carefully, she turned and went out of the kitchen.

Jake stood leaning against the counter thinking he could never again walk into this room without seeing Alexandra's face, flushed, alive with the challenge of battle, her hair moving around her head like a caramel cloud as they dueled with forks like silly kids, with nothing more at stake than their pride. For a little while, they'd forgotten everything, forgotten who and what they were, and that the world lay outside, waiting for them. But now she was going back into it alone. And he was doing nothing to stop her, nothing to lay claim to her, or make sure that she didn't forget what she had had with him. He was doing nothing to stop her from thinking she was to blame because two men had failed her.

Damn it to hell. Why couldn't he have been first with her?

He couldn't change the past. It was over, gone. They weren't kids anymore. They were adults and the time was right. They were right for each other. Didn't she know it? Couldn't she feel it? He ran an impatient hand through his hair. His instinct told him that if he did what he wanted to do, press and press hard, he'd scare her away. And if he did alienate her again, his chances of getting her back were zero.

The best thing he could do was nothing. But he didn't like to sit around and wait and hope. He liked to take action. He liked to think he made a difference in the world. And he would make a difference in the part of his world that mattered most. Alexandra. As soon as he figured out what in hell it was he should do.

In the bathroom, Alexandra picked up her damp clothes from where they lay on the floor, mute signs that they had been cast off quickly and carelessly. Her T-shirt was next to the sink, her bra in a corner by the bathtub. She fastened on the cold damp bra with shaking hands, the chilly clothes a distinct shock to her warmed, well-loved body. She should have been more sensible. She should have put her clothes in Jake's dryer. She should have gone home as soon as she'd finished tending his wound.

She shouldn't have made love with him.

But she had. That was why she was feeling vulnerable and confused . . . and alone.

She came out of the bathroom to find Jake slouched down on the couch, a glass of wine on the low glass-topped table in front of him. When she'd first entered the condo, she'd been so worried about him that she hadn't noticed the tasteful luxury of his home. Now she saw it suited him perfectly. Thick beige carpeting, glass and oak furniture with touches of brass. A saucy orange pillow on the couch, breaking the monochrome tastefulness of the matching chair. Opulent, but comfortable. Masculine, but beautiful. Like him.

When will I see you again?

She desperately wanted to ask the question, but her pride—and the look in his eyes—kept the words inside. Instead, she simply drank in the sight of him, the stark beauty of his face, the way the worn bathrobe clung to his hard, virile body. "You'd better have your nurse look at that gash on your head tomorrow morning. You lost your bandage while we were . . ." She trailed off, unable to finish the thought aloud, or inside her head.

"I'll do that," he said, his eyes meeting hers steadily. "Thanks for your concern."

There was no double entendre in his words. Just a polite dismissal. He twisted his head and remained sitting in the same position she'd found him in, staring at his wineglass.

"Anytime." She stood stock-still. There must be something she could say, something to destroy the wall that had risen between them simply because she had to go.

She took a step toward him. "Jake . . ." He lifted his eyes to hers.

Hell and damnation. What did she want, a goodbye kiss? If he touched her, he'd never let her out of that door. Not for the rest of the night. Or the rest of his life. Couldn't she just get the hell out?

The expression on his face was so icily calm that it chilled Alexandra to the bone. There wasn't a trace of her teasing caveman lover. He had the look of a man who couldn't wait for her to go. Her chin came up. "Goodbye," she said. Her head held high, she walked to the door, opened it, and went out, pulling it firmly closed behind her.

Jake brought his fist down on the glass-topped table. It held, but his wineglass wobbled unsteadily. Small satisfaction, he thought grimly. He lurched up off the couch and went into the bedroom. Mistake. The sheets were explicitly mussed, the pillow still wearing the imprint of her head.

He would never want another woman there. He knew it with an awful, searing certainty. He'd found his polestar, his other. What had Alexandra found? A pleasing diversion? An outlet for the sensuality that seemed to come as naturally to her as breathing?

Cursing, he went into the bathroom to take a shower.

THE WIND HAD DIED AWAY to a breeze but the sky was still studded with clouds that hid the stars when Alexandra ran lightly up the steps of her mother's house. Outside the door, she fumbled for her key, shivering, not from her damp clothes as much as from a surfeit of emotion. She seemed to have felt more things, done more things, been more things in this one short evening than in all the rest of her life.

The golden circle of light from the lamp her mother had left on waited for her. Unlike the night she'd left Kurt, the solitary beam evoked not loneliness, but a strange lift of the heart. Despite the way Jake had looked when she'd walked out the door, she was—at this moment—not quite as alone in the world as she had been. She'd had Jake as friend, dueling opponent—and lover. No matter what the future might hold, this night was hers to treasure, to take out and dust off and relive anytime she pleased.

Inside her room, stripping off her clothes, Alexandra remembered how being with Jake had made her feel. How he'd claimed her body...and her heart. While showering, she remembered. But when she came out of the bathroom in her robe, her hair wrapped in a towel, Katherine stood in the doorway, wearing a hurt look. Thoughts of Jake went flying from Alexandra's head.

"I heard you come in. I was still awake." Katherine looked so much younger in her light cotton nightgown, her cropped hair mussed. "Can I talk to you for a minute, or are you going right to bed?" She was fragile, on edge, vulnerable. She'd never come into Alexandra's room before, never asked for a private talk or anything else. All part of her determination not to be any more of a charity case than she felt she already was.

"Of course I have time. Sit down." Alexandra gestured toward her bed. Carefully keeping her eyes away from Katherine, trying to act as if her presence in the softly lit room was the most natural thing in the world, Alexandra went to her dresser and sat down in front of her mirror. She pulled the towel off her head and picked up a hairbrush to run through her wet hair. She had to act casually and take her cue from the girl.

"Did you and Jake have a good time tonight?"

Out of the mouths of babes. . . .

Alexandra's eyes flickered up to meet Katherine's in the mirror, searching the girl's face for a deeper meaning to her words, but not finding it. "Yes, we did."

Katherine lifted her chin a notch. "Are you two going to be a thing?"

Alexandra lowered the hairbrush. "What does that mean?"

Katherine shrugged her shoulders, impatient with the obtuse older generation. "It means going out and stuff."

"Possibly we will be 'going out and stuff.'" How could she tell Katherine what lay ahead with Jake when she hadn't a clue herself? "Will that bother you?" She might have expected this. Despite Katherine's struggle to remain detached from Jake, she seemed to have developed a young girl's jealousy.

"I thought you would . . . come home sooner. I was waiting for you."

Alexandra twisted around to face Katherine, thinking how much she'd wronged the girl. Katherine hadn't developed an adolescent jealousy for Jake. It was Alexandra's affection the teenager was afraid to share. And afraid to lose.

She stretched out to touch Katherine's shoulder, but the girl moved out of her reach to avoid her touch, just as she always had. As she always would unless Alexandra bridged the gap. Now. Tonight.

"I know you did, sweetheart. I'm sorry I couldn't come home right away."

The dark hurt in Katherine's eyes stirred a childhood memory in Alexandra. She remembered clearly how it felt to be a lonely, unhappy child and have an adult fail her. She rose and went to sit down on the bed beside Katherine, gathering up the girl's cold hands in hers. Katherine stiffened, but she didn't push her away. A small concession, but an important one. Carefully, lightly, Alexandra squeezed the girl's fingers.

"I didn't realize my not coming home as soon as you wanted me to would make you feel so lonely."

Alexandra's understanding brought the first glisten of tears to Katherine's eyes, but when she raised them to meet her aunt's, they were defiant. "How do you know what I felt?"

"I do, believe me. I remember very well being your age and having someone I loved let me down. I'm sorry I did that to you." She stroked Katherine's hand soothingly. "I'm sorry for so many things. I'm sorry you lost your parents, sorry you had to leave your friends and come live with me, sorry I wasn't here when you needed me tonight." Alexandra hesitated, took a breath, and plunged. "And most of all, I'm sorry you're afraid to love me or anybody else again."

Katherine's tears came then, at long, long last.

Alexandra hugged her hard and close. The girl clung to her with heartrending desperation. Alexandra patted her back in the timeworn comforting way. "We have to fight back, sweetheart. We can't just give up. We have to try and love again, even if we've been hurt terribly. Of all the crazy things in this crazy world, loving is all we have left to keep us sane." Yesterday she couldn't have said those words to Katherine. Yesterday she hadn't known the truth of them. Tonight, after being with Jake, she did.

Katherine burrowed into Alexandra's shoulder, a wounded animal seeking comfort. "I hate... being... such a baby, crying and stuff."

Alexandra smiled into the darkness, her own eyes glistening with tears. "You're not being a baby. You're being human." She pulled Katherine away to look into her face. "We do allow that around here occasionally, you know. But only on dark cloudy nights, when you can't see the moon, and there's lightning and thunder and the wind blows the cloud shadows over the trees."

"You're... crazy," Katherine managed to say between residual sniffles.

"There's a lot of that going around, too." Alexandra went on smiling and wiped a lock of hair away from Katherine's tear-stained cheek. Her smile faded and she studied Katherine with sober, adult seriousness. "I do know one thing. I'm crazy about you."

"You can't... like me after the way I've been." Sheepish, a little guilty, but far too intelligent to be lied to.

"You have been a prickly pear," Alexandra said. "But I couldn't stop loving you then, and I won't stop loving you now. I'll always love you, no matter what you say or do. You're part of me. I'm part of you. We're family. We belong together."

Katherine stared at Alexandra, a fierce love and pride glowing in her eyes, expanding to fill the emptiness. "You're not just saying that, are you?"

"Don't you know me well enough by now to know that I don't 'just say things?'"

"That was one of the things I liked about you from the first. You never lied to me and said it was going to be easy. You never tried to smooth things over by treating me like a baby and telling me everything was going to be all right. You've always been straight with me."

Alexandra gazed at her fondly. "So, you like me because I'm an honest woman?"

Katherine's eyes dropped. "Actually I . . . like everything about you. I like the way you look when you go to work in the morning, the way you take care of yourself, the way you take time to talk to me when I know you have work to do. Actually, I like you too much. I tried so hard not to. I was afraid . . . something would happen to you if I let myself think about how good you are to me and how much I like you."

The tears stung, but Alexandra found herself smiling. "Well, stop trying so hard to save my life with your big chill." She ruffled Katherine's hair. "What a superstitious little idiot you are. Nothing's going to happen to me. I'm going to live a long, happy life, throughout which I expect you to plague me with your presence...and your love. Especially your love. I need that most of all."

Katherine looked amazed. "You . . . need my love?"

"Absolutely. Who else do I have to look at to see my brother's awesome nose?"

With a small cry, Katherine launched herself against Alexandra and pulled her close with all the ferocity of her need and impetuous youth. Alexandra hugged back just as fiercely, her eyes and heart full of emotion.

9

THE ZONING BOARD MEETING was already in session when Alexandra slipped into her seat at the horseshoe-shaped table, very aware of being late. The meeting had begun promptly at seven-thirty p.m., as decreed by the board's secretary, First National's own Chas Gordon. It was now a quarter after eight. She'd be even more conscious of her lateness if Jake wasn't sitting just to her right dressed in a midnight-black tuxedo and a blindingly white shirt. He stood out like a celebrity in the midst of the other men who wore Florida casual, loose-fitting slacks and open-necked knit shirts. Lealda was dressed to the teeth of course, a match for Jake. Her red dress was pure silk, her shoulder scarf a blaze of tropical blues and yellows. On anyone else it would have looked outrageous. On Lealda it looked refined and classy.

Alexandra tried to avoid a clashing of eyes with Jake, but there was no escaping that shard-sharp green-eyed gaze. She felt more vulnerable than she thought possible, seeing him in public for the first time since they'd made love. Impossible not to look at his mouth and remember what he'd done to her with those shapely sensual lips. Impossible to look at his hands and not remember how skilled they were at lovemaking.

His face seemed more deeply tanned than she remembered, though it could hardly be so. Perhaps it was the contrast between the white and black that made him look so healthy and delectable. His jacket was hitched back to reveal his narrow waist defined by a cream silk cummerbund, his flat belly and hard thighs pressing against fine black wool.

Jake dipped his head slightly to her in greeting. Well accustomed to hiding her thoughts in public, she returned his nod with cool politeness. But her mind treacherously recreated the vivid memory of him, naked and gloriously aroused.

His eyes glinted with humor and sexual awareness, no doubt fueled by his memories of her wearing considerably less than the designer suit she had on. Disturbed by the tugging sensation in her lower body, she pulled her eyes away from him. But Jake stayed in Alexandra's mind, along with other devastating thoughts that centered on him. Why was he so dressed up? Where was he going?

Freed from the grip of his gaze and those first few seconds of intimacy they'd shared, her rapport with him vanished, driven away by his formal dress and the planned evening it implied. She felt oddly alienated from him, pushed out of his life. It was as if the other night hadn't happened. Her stomach tightened, her hands felt cold.

In the two days since she'd last seen him, he hadn't called. Nor had she called him. Nervous as a cat, she'd spent most of the day thinking about him, about herself, about her unwillingness to commit herself to him, and the parallels between her life and Katherine's. She'd exhorted Katherine to have the courage to love again. When she'd said the words, she realized with blinding clarity that she was the one who needed to take her own advice.

Alexandra knew she shouldn't be sitting in the meeting feeling like a lovesick teenager. She had to pay attention to what was going on.

What was going on was fraught with the potential for conflict. A couple was petitioning for permission to put what Alexandra knew was a too-big house on a too-small lot. Several of their neighbors had come to voice their concern and opposition to the plan.

Alexandra opened her briefcase and withdrew the yellow legal pad where she took her personal notes of the meeting. Before she could write a word, Jake leaned over, appropriated both pen and pad and wrote a note to her.

Why are you late?

His handwriting, like most doctors', could win no prizes. It was atrocious, always had been. She was one of the few people in the world who could read it. But he did deserve a prize for unadulterated nerve. What right did he have to inquire into her life when he was sitting there looking like Cary Grant on his way to a French embassy party?

She scrawled her answer, *I went out for a ride with Katherine, John Valentine, and his brother.*

He took the pen from her hand again, his fingers warm, evocative.

Was the brother tall enough for you?

She snatched the pad from his easy hold. *No, he was short but charming—very charming*, she emphasized.

Jake was no fool. He knew irritation when he saw it. He hadn't meant to annoy, only to tease. Gently, he eased the pad away from her fingers and scratched in his half-printed, mostly illegible scrawl, *You let Katherine go out with a boy?*

She was in a crowd that included me.

She's too young.

She'll be thirteen in a few more weeks, and this is the first time she wanted to go. I thought it was a good sign.

Her long years of business expertise helped her control the sharp tingles of anger. She'd been so eager to tell Jake about her talk with Katherine, to share with him her excitement about her breakthrough with the girl. Jake had been a part of that breakthrough and he deserved to share in the victory. Instead, he was giving her the third degree about Katherine's new growth without any of the background.

Are you sure you know what you're doing?

Probably not. But I'm doing it anyway. She paused, then after Jake's eyes had traveled over the words, she was driven to scrawl, *I take it you think I'm making a serious mistake encouraging her interest in boys?*

His expression noncommittal, he shook his head and made no move to reach for the pad to answer her. He shifted in the chair, bringing his shoulder closer to hers. Dear heaven, what scent was he wearing? It was wonderful, very masculine, as suggestive and enticing as old cedarwood.

Desire—sweet, hot, and unwanted—stirred, fueling her energy and her courage. She was not in the mood to be enticed. Or want a man who was going out with another woman. Driven by a recklessness she'd already manifested in the past ten years, she took the pad and wrote, *You certainly smell good.*

Thank you kindly, ma'am, he wrote accenting the words with a long, scrawled underline.

Casually, she retrieved the pad. The recklessness was still riding her. He'd asked his questions, gotten his answers. Now it was her turn.

Why are you so dressed up?

He read what she'd written, lifted a lazy brow and smiled a maddening smile at her.

Going out afterward.

Well, she'd wanted an answer and she'd got it, succinct but not very informative. Only her pride kept her from scrawling, *Who's the lucky woman?*

She flicked a sidelong glance at him. He'd turned his attention back to the meeting, his smooth well-groomed jaw perfectly controlled, his body still with attentive politeness.

As if she didn't exist. Or matter. Her anger warmed her cheeks, made her eyes sparkle. Suddenly self-conscious about both the way she was looking at him as well as her inattentiveness, Alexandra lifted her head to turn her attention to the meeting—and found Lealda studying her with the gleeful joy of a miner appraising a nugget of gold.

Jake took the pad and wrote, *You're blushing, love.*

Alexandra shook her head. The game was no longer any fun. She didn't want to think about Jake looking the way he did, smelling the way he did, calling her his "love" and then going out to meet another woman. She'd come here, resolving to speak to him, to tell him that helping Katherine grow up had made her grow up, too. She'd yearned to see him again and try to undo the damage she'd done. But finding Jake dressed to kill, busy with a life of his own that excluded her, shook both her resolve and her self-confidence.

Maybe she'd misunderstood him and their night together, given it too much significance. Maybe she was nothing more than an enjoyable interlude to him. Maybe he'd never meant for them to have anything more than a night of casual sex.

Alexandra didn't want to feel this way, confused, storm-tossed. Not about Jake. He'd been the one reliable male in her life, honest to the point of bluntness, a pole of unvarying stability, a man she could always rely on to mean what he said, a man who'd never, as long as she'd known him, given out false signals.

Most important of all, he'd never let her down.

She couldn't bear it if he turned out to be like all the rest. Maybe that was what she was really afraid of. She'd respected Jake all her life. If he destroyed that respect, that esteem she had for him alone, she would have no anchor left in her world. There would be no one she could believe in. Not even herself. Maybe that was her real problem in committing herself to Jake.

"Ms Holden, your area of expertise is waterfront property," said Chas Gordon. "I'd like to hear your opinion on this petition."

Caught, Alexandra glanced down at the paper containing the information about the house they were being asked to consider. She had studied the material during her lunch hour and she knew the neighborhood well, but every thought on her mind seemed to have abandoned her. She gave herself a minute to clear her mind, then directed her gaze at the petitioning couple. The woman seemed to be the more aggressive of the pair. The man was rotund, red-faced, amiable, and obviously embarrassed by the conflict.

Jake relaxed back in the chair and got ready to enjoy himself. Alexandra might have been writing notes to him and only half attending to the proceedings, but if he knew his lady, and he did, she'd give a succinct and organized presentation of the facts and the reasons why no variance could be allowed. And she would deliver it in a calm inoffensive tone.

Which is precisely what she did. Alexandra spoke of the inherent dangers of building too close to the water, the problem of landscaping a house that was too big for the lot, the need for a new home to fit into the rest of the community without impeding the neighbor's view of the sea. She spoke of the board's responsibility to uphold the standards of the whole community, to look beyond the needs of the moment and to remember that the decisions they made now would impact upon the future.

"All your points are well taken," said Chas Gordon. "Dr. Hustead, do you have anything to add?"

Alexandra moved in her chair, too good a business executive to let her annoyance show on her face. But Jake knew.

"Ms Holden has covered the ground extremely well. The only thing I could add is that I think Mr. and Mrs. Chelsey haven't thought about how much they might want more yard space. They tell us their children are grown and gone, but children tend to get married and bring home their own little ones who'd need a place to play outside."

"An excellent point, Doctor."

"It seems to me that a house could be designed to adequately meet the needs of two people and still remain within the restrictions of the standard ordinance."

"But we've spent so much money having these plans drawn up," the woman protested.

"I'm sorry you'll have incurred the extra expense," Jake said gently, "but what we've suggested is your best course of action."

A unified front. It felt odd to be facing conflict, with Jake on her side. It felt . . . good.

There were other items on the agenda, but Alexandra found it hard to keep her attention focused on them as the meeting dragged on. At last, a little before ten o'clock, Chas Gordon called for a vote of adjournment. Jake quickly obliged him.

In the hallway, Jake came up behind her and caught her elbow. "You're in a hurry tonight."

She turned and with deliberate nonchalance, ran an inspecting gaze over him. "Aren't you?"

"Not particularly. I told Rob I'd be there when I got there."

One delicate pale eyebrow lifted. "You don't look dressed to go out with a 'Rob.'"

"Who do I look dressed to go out with?"

"I'd say at the very least a 'Valerie.' At the most, a 'Jacqueline.'"

The devil had the audacity to look pleased. "Are you jealous, woman o'mine?" He ran a teasing finger down her cheek and under her jaw.

"I'm not *your* woman."

His teasing smile faded. His eyes darkened and his grip on her arm tightened. Before she quite knew what was happening, she was pushed forward and then sideways into another meeting room. Jake flipped on the light and slammed the door closed.

"What are you do—"

He trundled her up against the closed door and captured her between his body and the hard wood. His steady gaze was a force to be reckoned with, sweeping over her face with a new intensity. This was Jake in possession, a side of him she hadn't seen in all the years she'd known him.

"I thought we'd settled that question the other night."

"Is that what you thought?" He pressed his body against her, hard, heated, intimate. And yet he remained distant. He wore a cool removed expression, his sensual mouth sober, as if he was unaffected by her presence. She knew differently. His arousal nudged against her abdomen, initiating the delicious tingling that was, by now, so familiar to her.

He was exciting, surprising, marvelously, endlessly fascinating—this chameleon man she thought she knew and didn't. She shouldn't have liked his strangely cool possession. But she did. It was exhilarating to be locked intimately against a man who was so much in control of himself. "Maybe you were wrong," she said in a denial, lifting her sparkling eyes to his, her face alive with challenge, inviting him to lose his coolness.

"I don't . . . think so." He bent his head, but instead of kissing her with the same hard pressure his body exerted on hers, he teased her mouth with the lightest of kisses, a feathery brush of his lips that made her body leap to life with demands for more.

Her hands found his hips, but she couldn't press him closer. He was as close as he could be. But she could take possession and she did, cupping her hands on his high, hard buttocks.

"You keep doing that, lady, and I won't be going anywhere . . . except into you."

"Jake . . ."

He liked her like this, soft, yielding, sensually charged, slightly confused, her lips apart. He took a taste of her mouth, and then another and another. He was just thinking of forgetting the dinner with his associate when his pocket pager began to sound with its incessant, harshly intruding beep.

Even while he reached inside his tuxedo jacket to shut off the signal, she eased his body away from hers. He let her push him away, his eyes dark and knowing. In the silence, he stared down at her. "That was the reason I didn't ask you to go with me tonight. The dinner is for Rob and his fiancée. For him to be free, I have to be on call."

"I understand."

He caught her chin with his hand and tilted her face up to his. "Do you?"

She reached out to him, her hand hovering over his upper arm, then touching, making contact. "Yes." Her silvery-blue eyes locked with his. "You didn't have to go to such lengths to protect me from disappointment." In the quiet room, a clock ticked. "I'm not a child," she told him. "Not . . . anymore. I would have understood and accepted the interruption."

Jake knew what the words meant. She was telling him she'd come to terms with his career and who he was.

"But you didn't trust me enough to ask me to go with you," Alexandra said softly. "Maybe I'm not the only one who needs to learn to trust."

Groaning, he pulled her close and buried his mouth in the silken fall of her hair. "Next time, I'll trust you like hell."

Gently, she pushed him away, but her love for him shone brightly in her eyes. "I know," she said softly.

He read the calm acceptance in her face and his heart soared. His green eyes brilliant with joy, he caught her hand. "Walk me out to the parking lot?"

ON A CLOUDLESS NIGHT the following weekend, Jake lay in his bed beside Alexandra, his hand tracing idly over her bare abdomen. "You haven't told me about Katherine."

She raised a languid hand to his face, her eyes dark, her throat flushed with the loving that had gone before, and traced the bones of his face with a fingertip that he'd kissed and sucked—just as he had every other part of her. "Katherine who?"

He smiled, his lips curving suggestively. "Decadent, love. Thoroughly disgraceful." He leaned over and brushed his mouth on the crest of a still sensitive breast. "What libertine activities have you been engaging in to make you forget all your responsibilities?"

Her eyes darkened and to Jake's regret, she lost a bit of the sultry sensuality he'd spent half the night wrapping her in—and that looked so good on her. "Is it really possible to live like this, to have a little part of your life that is sacrosanct, to forget everything for a little while and just . . . feel?"

"It's possible, love." Her shoulder was too enticing. He leaned over and nibbled lazily. He should have been sated with her, but he was finding that a difficult state to achieve. After the loving, she was as uninhibited as a pagan princess, lush and erotic enough to tempt a saint. But he was no saint.

"I have to go to Hawaii next weekend," she announced flatly. He'd been wandering toward her throat but her words stopped him cold. He leaned over her, suspended between the chase and withdrawal.

Brilliant blue eyes sought out his. Had he known her less well, he might have suspected her of setting a trap for him. But there was no guile in her face, only a stark vulnerability that made his gut tighten and his throat fill. *I have my pocket pager, too,* she was saying. *Is it all right? Can you handle it?*

He dipped his head and placed his mouth to her throat, as if he was only intent on reawakening her. "When are you leaving?"

"Friday morning."

"I'll clear my schedule and drive you to the airport."

"That isn't necessary—"

Jake moved his body over hers and nudged his hungry hardness into her softness. She took him into her already fulfilled body, feeling the first stirrings of desire as he filled her emptiness. "I want to see you off."

He was creating a fullness, a heaviness in her, a need to give. "You . . . certainly have . . . unusual methods of persuasion, Doctor."

His eyes darkened as she raised her hips to meet his and her hunger drove her to intensify the slow, primitive rhythm. His mouth lifted in a beautifully sensual smile. "But you must admit they are effective."

"Most . . . effective." She reached up to pull him down for the kiss that awaited him.

Later, Alexandra propped herself up on her elbow to look at the time on his radio clock and spied the brandy snifter, which contained what looked like dried flower petals inside.

"What is that, Jake?"

"Your roses." He flipped back the sheet and padded to the bathroom. She sat contemplating the man who had saved the petals from the roses she'd given him and put them into a potpourri by his bedside.

ALEXANDRA THOUGHT of those roses when she stood with Jake outside the Miami airport in the heat. They were all she was leaving with him physically, but when he parked in the unloading zone and took out her luggage, she felt as if she were leaving her heart and soul behind with him.

It was all wrong to tell a man goodbye on a sidewalk crowded with redcaps and people, when that man's eyes were as dark with love, respect, and longing as Jake's were. He was missing her already. And she him. "You don't have to go inside with me," she said. "I'll only be in the airport a few minutes before boarding."

The wry expression on his face acknowledged the truth of her words.

"Thanks so much for bringing me." Her chin came up. She wanted to say, *This is the real world, Jake. That other world where you and I were for a little while is a dream. It can't last. What's worse, maybe our feelings for each other won't last. When I come back, you'll have had some experience that will make you feel slightly different about me. Or I'll act like a stranger with you because of the new experiences I've had. That's what time and distance does. It kills love.*

And then, looking as if he knew exactly what she was thinking, Jake touched her—casually, just a hand clasping her neck. "Come home safely to me," he murmured and pulled her close to receive his kiss. And suddenly, his mouth was the real world and everything else was a dream.

Jake took her back through all of it, made her remember with his hard body and demanding mouth what they'd had together. When he pulled away, he favored her with that male, possessive look. Bedroom eyes. Pleasure they'd had, pleasure they would have again. Alexandra was filled with a rush of heat that banished every worry from her head. He said softly, "Call me when you get there."

She fought to regain her equilibrium after the onslaught of his kiss, and from his fiery gaze. "It will be the middle of the night before—"

His eyes were knowing. "I won't be sleeping. Not until I hear that you've arrived safely."

Jake meant every word, she knew. He would worry about her. Because he cared. And didn't mind telling her he cared. Could she be any less brave? She stood for a moment consuming him with her eyes and then, unable to stop herself, she closed the gap between them and pulled him close. "I . . . love you, Jake."

He looked as if she'd dealt him a blow. Then, his hands tightened on her back and he pulled her into a hug that made no secret of his need for her. "Hell of a time to tell me." He pushed her away to look into her face. "I love you, too. Always have." He looked as surprised by his words as she felt hearing them. A heartbeat of silence went by. "Always will."

Alexandra raised her hand to his cheek. "You stay safe."

"Count on it," he said with heartfelt intensity.

IT WAS A SHOCK TO ARRIVE in Hawaii, both physically and mentally. Alexandra was accustomed to warm weather and tropical breezes, but she was not accustomed to the casual dress, the bare skin, the brilliant flowers, the relaxed, pleasure-seeking people of all sizes, shapes and colors. And the cleanliness. Everything was so sparkling clean. Thousands of tourists passed through these islands daily, yet there was not a scrap of litter anywhere.

At the hotel, a handsome dark-skinned young man came across the opulent gold and white lobby to take her bag. He escorted her to her room on the seventh floor of the luxurious building that would, if all went well, be one-tenth hers when she flew back to the States.

Her meeting was scheduled for the next day at one o'clock. She'd been warned that it might run into the wee hours while the feint and dance of negotiation went on.

Her hands trembling, she unpacked the three linen suits she'd brought, hung one in the bathroom to steam out when she showered and the other two in the closet. She was stressed out from jet lag, she told herself, but she knew that wasn't the only reason she felt shaky.

Alexandra Holden, the heart-whole and efficient business executive, the woman determined not to get involved with any man whose career was as demanding as her own, had burned her bridges. There was no way out. She'd told Jake she loved him and he'd told her he loved her. They were deeply involved with each other, committed to a love affair which would, eventually, come to an end.

Still, a part buried deep within her struggled to hope, to believe that there might be some way they could stay together forever.

Forever. She'd judiciously avoided thinking about forever. Until now. Saying goodbye to Jake at the airport had made her realize she didn't want to leave him without being sure that she could return to his arms. She didn't want to be plagued with thoughts about time and distance killing love. She wanted to be sure he would lay in no woman's arms until she returned. She wanted to know he was hers alone.

She was feeling possessive about him, utterly, totally possessive. Possessive enough to want his ring on her finger. That was what made her hands tremble as she walked back and forth between her suitcase and her bed, hanging up clothes and arranging her toiletries in the bathroom.

She was afraid to believe, afraid to hope. She'd believed and hoped so many times before only to have all her dreams explode in her face. She'd had one marriage to a dedicated man, and it had been an utter disaster. Could she bear to try again—and risk failing a second time?

She was swept by an urgent need to hear his voice. It would be late there and she really shouldn't call him now. That logical, reasonable thought didn't seem to prevent her from sitting on the bed and reaching for the phone. . . .

He sounded husky, but he wasn't asleep, or so he assured her. He asked her if she'd had a good flight—she told him yes. She asked him if he'd had a good trip home—he said no, it was too quiet in the car.

"And it's too quiet in my bed," he added in a dark tone that sent a chill radiating up her spine. There were memories in that tone, memories of shared whispers and cries and shouts of pleasure. She slid one nyloned leg over the other and tried to sit up a little straighter on the bed in a vain attempt to fend off the warmth curling in her abdomen.

"It better be just as quiet in yours," he grumbled.

She smiled at his tone, smiled at his insecurity, smiled at the ridiculous effect the sound of his voice had on her, especially since it was coming from several thousands of miles away. "The only sighs you'll hear in my bedroom are those from the surf."

He was silent for a moment, as if he too was remembering other sounds, other sighs. "I have this uncontrollable urge to go out in the kitchen," he said, "crack open a bottle of olives and share it with a woman who's got a mean right with a fork."

"Sounds dangerous to me."

"I'm a man who likes to live on the edge." A silence. "You aren't by any chance missing me a little, are you?"

"There's no chance to it. I'm missing you a lot."

"Still love me?" He asked so lightly, that her heart melted.

"More than ever."

"Hold that thought," he said huskily. "How long did you say it was until you come home? One light-year? Or two?"

"One, I think. Jake, when I get home—"

He quickly interrupted her. "Just concentrate on your merger, love. When you've got that settled and you can come home, we'll talk."

After a soft, unsatisfactory exchange of long distance kisses, and a reluctant goodbye, she hung up the phone and steeled herself to finish her unpacking.

Alexandra closed her suitcase, shoved it in the closet and carried her briefcase to the rectangular desk by the window. She could ease her worries about her future with Jake with a good four hours of work. She might be a failure in her personal relationships, but in her career she had no such doubts, no sense of failure to ease. Whatever else happened, she was secure in the knowledge that she had never failed in her career. This hotel investiture was the culmination of all she'd worked for. It would announce to the world her success as a woman entrepreneur.

Still, she could take nothing for granted. She needed to be thoroughly prepared for the meeting tomorrow. The investment group had all but assured her they were willing to accept her money, but nothing was certain until the contracts were signed. There still could be rough waters ahead.

Very rough waters, she thought the next day when she took her place at the oval table among the men who were seated there. She and the woman who was acting as secretary were the only two females in the room.

Before they were too many minutes into the meeting, it became apparent that her chief opponent was Walter Hennings, a banker from New York City. During the meeting, he seemed polite enough, but afterward, when they'd agreed to take a coffee break, and they rose from their chairs to mingle more informally with each other, he threaded through the clusters of men toward her. Mentally, Alexandra braced herself.

He was a tall, handsome man with a thick mane of white hair. He looked as if he'd never had the word "no" spoken to him in his life. "I've looked over the brochure you prepared on your company's assets, Ms Holden. Quite impressive. Unusual for a daughter to take over a father's business and make it even more . . . lucrative."

"I'm surprised you think it so unusual." Alexandra forced herself to meet his gaze steadily but without rancor. She'd learned long ago that she couldn't change the world. Male chauvinists were becoming few in number, but the species was still not extinct.

"I was inclined to veto your inclusion in the group."

"Were you?" Only someone who knew her well would have seen the storm signals lighting up her silvery eyes.

"Women tend to be such capricious creatures, sure of something one minute and ready to change their mind the next."

"While men rarely suffer the pangs of indecision." The words were cool, polite, and to an undiscerning, unsuspecting ear like Hennings's meant only that she was agreeing with him.

"Men do study a situation carefully and examine all the angles before they commit themselves."

"Yes, I've always thought men were rather good at angling." She gave him a pleasant smile, but Hennings frowned as if, for the first time, he'd caught a hint of the double meaning in her words. Before he could react, she put out her hand. "I'm so glad you acted without prejudice and allowed me to be a part of the group, Mr. Hennings. I'm sure your wife is proud of you."

He shook her hand and while he was still staring at her with a startled expression, she said smoothly, "Excuse me. I'd like to go and have some of that coffee."

10

"HENNINGS IS a male chauvinist," Alexandra told Jake on the phone that night, as she lay in bed in her empire-style nightie, the only covering she needed in the air-conditioned room.

"Is he indeed?" Jake's drawl was indulgent. She wished he was there beside her now, touching her, loving her. She wanted to see that sensual smile curl his lips, wanted to see his green eyes darken with sexual hunger, wanted to see his strong beautiful body come alive with need for her.

"I've no doubt you'll soon set him to rights."

"How are things with you?"

The pause was infinitesimal, but she heard it. "Fine," he said at last.

"Jake, don't lie to me."

Another pause, deliberate this time. Then he said huskily, "I miss you."

"I miss you, too. This bed seems as big as a football field without you in it."

"I wouldn't mind being there with you to . . . score a few touchdowns."

She smiled. "I'd cheer you on."

"Something you do with infinite skill, love."

She remembered touchdowns he'd scored, the cheering on she'd done. The remembering turned her hot, edgy, needy. "I think we'd better talk about something else."

"I *know* we'd better talk about something else." His devilish drawl told her he was feeling just what she was feeling.

"Did you go sailing with Katherine this afternoon?"

"Nope. She had other plans. She was going out for ice cream with Johnny, his brother and another girl. If I didn't mind too much. I told her I didn't mind as long as she had your permission to go. She said she did."

"I talked to her during my dinner break. She's healing, Jake. Thanks to you."

"Hey, let's not kid ourselves. It was your persistence that finally did the trick. I'm proud of you, love."

"Thanks." She felt as if he'd given her a pound of diamonds. "If things keep moving along as well as they have been, I'll be able to get out of here on Tuesday as planned."

"Three whole days. I'm not sure I can wait."

The sexual teasing was gone from his voice. He sounded cool, matter-of-fact. A few minutes later when she hung up the phone, Alexandra lay back in bed and stared up at the ceiling. Why did she feel so uneasy? He'd said all the right things, including a whispered, "I'm going crazy without you, love. Hurry home," at the end of their conversation. But there was a dark edge in his voice that made her think he was holding something back. What?

The peach shades of dawn lent a pearly glow to her drapes, telling her it was early morning when the phone rang. She came awake instantly, her heart pounding, the adrenaline flowing through her veins. "Hello?"

A heavy silence answered her. "Hello?" She clutched the receiver, not sure whether she was getting a crank call or an honest wrong number.

"I had to hear your voice," a guttural mumble said in her ear.

"Jake?" She twisted around and sat on the edge of the bed, the blood pounding in her ears.

"I needed to know you were still in the world. I'm sorry. I shouldn't have called. You don't need me crying on your shoulder just now."

She'd known something was wrong. "Jake, what is it?"

"Little Yosheko is gone. Who was it that said the good die young?"

The grieving cynicism in his words hurt too much. She sagged into herself, trying to deal with the pain. "Jake. I'm . . . so sorry."

"Aren't we all?" There was a deep irony in his voice, a sardonic abandonment of hope.

"Are you at the condo? You shouldn't be alone. Go to your mother's house, let her be with you, please, darling."

"I wouldn't push my company on anybody just now, least of all my mother."

Hurting for him and for herself because she wasn't there to comfort him, Alexandra closed her eyes. He was a stubborn, proud man and she loved every bit of him, even his stubborn pride.

"I've got a bottle, baby. It will have to do until you come home."

"Jake, please don't drink. You need to be with some-one—"

"Yeah. I need to be with you. But you're on the other side of the bloody, damn world. On your way home, keep that plane up in the air, lady. I'm not in the mood to lose any more people I love."

The phone clicked in her ear.

She ached to call him back. If she did, what would she say to him? He wasn't in the mood to listen.

She lay in bed with nothing but the gentle hum of the air conditioning to keep her company. And her disturbing thoughts. She had plenty of those.

She stared up at the ceiling, torn by despair, desolate with her pain for Jake, desperately wanting to be with him. He needed her now, not three days from now.

He would survive. He was an adult, he was a doctor, he was used to dealing with pain and death. But her mind's eye replaced the picture of Jake out on the sailboard, defying the wind and the ocean with the strength of his own body to find victory over an unfathomably cruel fate. He would survive, yes. But he would survive far better if she was there beside him.

Think, her mind pleaded. Think what you're giving up if you leave without staying to sign the contract. Your credibility will be out the window with these people. Hennings will be smugly reassured that he knew all along you were a capricious woman. There's too much at stake—your reputation, your career, your opportunity to make more money in one year than you have in ten. He will be all right until you get home. . . .

Her father must have thought exactly the same thing. He'd made the choices that massaged his ego and ensured his financial success and his status in the business community.

She was faced with the same choice. She could stay and do what she'd planned to do and reap financial rewards and acclaim, possibly even approbation from Chas Gordon, a sign she had indeed made it to the top. If she left Hawaii before she signed the contract, she would, for the first time in her life, fail at her career.

And if she returned home and her love affair with Jake failed, she would be left with nothing.

Alexandra was beginning to understand why her father had chosen his career. That was the safe choice.

It could be hers.

But if she made that choice, if she, after all these years, emulated her father and became what she hated, how could she face Jake? How could she say she loved him without feeling like she was telling the biggest lie of her life?

She didn't have to be like her father.

Alexandra lunged out of bed and hustled to the closet to yank out her suitcase.

An hour later she was dressed, downstairs and handing the sleepy desk clerk a bulky manila envelope. "Would you give this to Mr. Hennings, please? And order me a taxi?"

At the airport, Alexandra had trouble booking out on the first plane to Miami. She took a chance, agreed to fly standby, and by some miracle, her name was called.

The flight back seemed endless. As she neared the Miami airport, her anxiety level rose. She tried to sleep but she was too keyed up.

When she'd claimed her luggage and stepped out into the hot wind to get into her rental car, exhaustion rolled over her in waves. Alexandra set her chin at a determined angle, slid into the car and fastened her seat belt in preparation for the four-hour drive ahead of her.

At six-thirty in the morning, she stood in the golden sunrise and then plucked the extra key out from under the flowerpot, letting herself into Jake's condo. Inside, the silence was deafening. The only thing she could hear was the thumping of her heart.

She ventured into Jake's bedroom. His suit jacket and pants were scattered on the bed they had shared, along with his shirt and tie. His running shoes were gone from the closet.

He'd obviously slept in his clothes, then changed for a jog on the beach.

Anxiously aware of the butterflies holding footraces in her stomach, she ran out of the condo and looked right, then left. He was running away from the dawn, a small figure retreating farther and farther down the beach.

Alexandra kicked off her high-heeled pumps, hiked up her skirt and began to run after him. She'd never won a race with Jake in her life, but she had to win this one.

He wasn't running fast but she could see the back of his hair was soaked with perspiration. He must have been at it for a while.

"Jake!"

He didn't hear her. She put her head down and put on a spurt of speed, pounding over the sand. "Jake!"

He turned then and saw her. He looked drawn with fatigue, his skin stretched over the hard bones of his face and gleaming with sweat, like a man intent on driving himself to the limits of his endurance.

Tenderness rose up and engulfed her. She needed to touch him.

His bleak expression stopped her in her tracks. His eyes flared with surprise as they took in the sight of her, but his face was cool, almost disbelieving.

"What are you doing here?"

It was not the reception she'd expected.

"I came back because . . . you needed me."

He didn't deny it. Nor did he confirm it.

Alexandra's heart pounded with trepidation. Jake appeared not to care where she was—or where he was.

She took a step closer to him, her nylon-stockinged feet catching in the sand. "I wanted to tell you how sorry I am about Yosheko."

He stared at her for another long moment. "Yeah, we were all sorry." An impatient hand came up to swipe at the damp hair falling over his forehead, as if he wanted to distract her from the harsh grief on his face. "What about your contract? Aren't you missing out on the signing?"

"I gave it up."

For the first time, a hint of interest enlivened his face. "You walked out? Just like that?"

"Just like that."

"Why?"

"Why?" The man was on his feet, he seemed to be awake. How could he be so dense? "Because you need me here."

He didn't move toward her. He just stood there looking at her, making her feel chilled and foolish.

"You could have stayed. I didn't ask you to come back."

"I know you didn't. All the more reason for me to come."

"Don't do this to me, Alexandra," he said. Her heart chilled at his use of her formal name after all she'd been through. "Don't make sacrifices for me that you will hate me for afterward."

"All this talk about hating you afterward. You must think I'm very... capricious."

He gazed at her steadily. "Maybe I love you so damned much that I'm scared to death I'll do something that will make you walk out of my life."

Alexandra stared at him. As self-assured and arrogant as he had always seemed to her, Jake was, at the moment, oddly insecure and vulnerable.

She hadn't known he could be so vulnerable. When she thought of the thousands of wonderful new things there were to learn about Jake, her heart swelled with joy. She could spend a lifetime studying him and never completely understand the depth of his intellect and emotions. But what fun it was going to be to try.

Lightly, her eyes lifting to his, she said, "I have no intention of walking out of your life. I gave up a contract for you. I don't know what more I can do to prove I love you with all my heart."

Alexandra made her declaration with a husky sincerity intensified by the sound of ocean breeze. How beautiful she looked standing there with her heart in her eyes. No, it wasn't in her eyes. She'd placed it in his keeping. He had the rest of his life to take very, very good care of it. He'd see to that.

How did Alexandra know instantly that her words had had their effect on him? Was it the slight quirking of Jake's mouth? Or that sudden flash of emotion in his eyes? Or that subtle change in his body language?

"Oh, there is one more thing you can do. You can marry me."

The words were flat, cool. She doubted if there had ever been a more unromantic proposal made to a woman anywhere.

She lifted her chin. "When?"

"Tonight. Tomorrow. As soon as it can be arranged."

She loved his impetuousness, his zest for life, his gutsy reaching for what he wanted. Especially when what he wanted was her. Still, it might be wise to try to be reasonable. If she could. "Jake, you don't know what you're asking. There's your career and mine, and Katherine. We should probably wait a little longer, let everybody have time to get used to the idea...."

"Katherine's healing. As for our careers, you gave up an important business deal to come to me. How could I do any less for you? I'll always be there for you."

Joy spread through her. He meant it, as no man in her life ever had. And she believed him, as she never had any other man.

Jake stood watching her, his brilliant green eyes shining. "We can work it out, Alex."

She met his eyes fearlessly. "I never doubted it for a minute."

"Does this mean you're my woman?"

"That's what it means... as long as you agree to be my man."

He tried to appear unmoved, but his eyes darkened fractionally. "Is that an acceptance of my proposal, Ms Holden?"

"Yes, Dr. Hustead. Now, I'd like a welcome home kiss, please." She lifted demure eyes to him.

"How enticing the lady can be when she wants something," Jake said smoothly.

"Oh, the lady wants something, all right."

"What does she want?" Jake pretended to be blandly unmoved.

"The lady wants... you."

He tipped his head to the sky and said, "Demanding little hussy, isn't she? Maybe I should cool her off."

He came and conquered, reaching under her legs and snatching her up into his arms. His self-assurance restored, he walked purposefully with her to the edge of the ocean.

She settled herself against his chest in a comfortable spot in his arms and looked up into his face with complacence.

His brow furrowed in puzzled surprise. "No kicking, no screaming, no complaining about your designer skirt? No telling me you don't have time to play?"

Her silvery blue eyes looked up into his and they were so clear and true that his heart kicked over in his breast.

"If you're going into the ocean, I'm going with you. Wherever you go, I go."

His look of stunned surprise pleased her. He looked shaken to the soles of his sandy shoes by her deep faith in him. But being Jake, his recovery was quick. A soft moan escaped his throat and he lowered his head and captured her mouth with his. "I do love you too much," she said. "You're going to have to love me a lot just to put up with me."

"I might...be able to manage that...with a little help from you."

He swung her away from the water, set her down on her feet, and with his eyes on hers, extended his hand.

Alexandra slipped her fingers into his and with him at her side, turned to face the dawn. Their faces illuminated by the rising sun, they walked toward the beginning of a new day—and the life they would share—together.

Take 4 bestselling love stories FREE

Plus get a FREE surprise gift!

Special Limited-time Offer

Harlequin Reader Service®

Mail to

In the U.S.
3010 Walden Avenue
P.O. Box 1867
Buffalo, N.Y. 14269-1867

In Canada
P.O. Box 609
Fort Erie, Ontario
L2A 5X3

YES! Please send me 4 free Harlequin Temptations® novels and my free surprise gift. Then send me 4 brand-new novels every month, which I will receive months before they appear in bookstores. Bill me at the low price of $2.39* each—a savings of 26¢ apiece off cover prices. There are no shipping, handling or other hidden costs. I understand that accepting the books and gift places me under no obligation ever to buy any books. I can always return a shipment and cancel at any time. Even if I never buy another book from Harlequin, the 4 free books and the surprise gift are mine to keep forever.

*Offer slightly different in Canada—$2.39 per book plus 49¢ per shipment for delivery. Sales tax applicable in N.Y.

342 BPA ZDHU (CAN)

142 BPA MDX5 (US)

Name	(PLEASE PRINT)	
Address		Apt. No.
City	State/Prov.	Zip/Postal Code

This offer is limited to one order per household and not valid to present Harlequin Temptation® subscribers. Terms and prices are subject to change.

© 1990 Harlequin Enterprises Limited

PASSPORT TO ROMANCE
SWEEPSTAKES RULES

1. **HOW TO ENTER:** To enter, you must be the age of majority and complete the official entry form, or print your name, address, telephone number and age on a plain piece of paper and mail to: Passport to Romance, P.O. Box 9056, Buffalo, NY 14269-9056. No mechanically reproduced entries accepted.

2. All entries must be received by the CONTEST CLOSING DATE, DECEMBER 31, 1990 TO BE ELIGIBLE.

3. **THE PRIZES:** There will be ten (10) Grand Prizes awarded, each consisting of a choice of a trip for two people from the following list:
   i) London, England (approximate retail value $5,050 U.S.)
   ii) England, Wales and Scotland (approximate retail value $6,400 U.S.)
   iii) Carribean Cruise (approximate retail value $7,300 U.S.)
   iv) Hawaii (approximate retail value $9,550 U.S.)
   v) Greek Island Cruise in the Mediterranean (approximate retail value $12,250 U.S.)
   vi) France (approximate retail value $7,300 U.S.)

4. Any winner may choose to receive any trip or a cash alternative prize of $5,000.00 U.S. in lieu of the trip.

5. **GENERAL RULES:** Odds of winning depend on number of entries received.

6. A random draw will be made by Nielsen Promotion Services, an independent judging organization, on January 29, 1991, in Buffalo, NY, at 11:30 a.m. from all eligible entries received on or before the Contest Closing Date.

7. Any Canadian entrants who are selected must correctly answer a time-limited, mathematical skill-testing question in order to win.

8. Full contest rules may be obtained by sending a stamped, self-addressed envelope to: "Passport to Romance Rules Request", P.O. Box 9998, Saint John, New Brunswick, Canada E2L 4N4.

9. Quebec residents may submit any litigation respecting the conduct and awarding of a prize in this contest to the Régie des loteries et courses du Québec.

10. Payment of taxes other than air and hotel taxes is the sole responsibility of the winner.

11. Void where prohibited by law.

COUPON BOOKLET OFFER TERMS

To receive your Free travel-savings coupon booklets, complete the mail-in Offer Certificate on the preceeding page, including the necessary number of proofs-of-purchase, and mail to: Passport to Romance, P.O. Box 9057, Buffalo, NY 14269-9057. The coupon booklets include savings on travel-related products such as car rentals, hotels, cruises, flowers and restaurants. Some restrictions apply. The offer is available in the United States and Canada. Requests must be postmarked by January 25, 1991. Only proofs-of-purchase from specially marked "Passport to Romance" Harlequin® or Silhouette® books will be accepted. The offer certificate must accompany your request and may not be reproduced in any manner. Offer void where prohibited or restricted by law. LIMIT FOUR COUPON BOOKLETS PER NAME, FAMILY, GROUP, ORGANIZATION OR ADDRESS. Please allow up to 8 weeks after receipt of order for shipment. Enter quickly as quantities are limited. Unfulfilled mail-in offer requests will receive free Harlequin® or Silhouette® books (not previously available in retail stores), in quantities equal to the number of proofs-of-purchase required for Levels One to Four, as applicable.

PR-SWPS

OFFICIAL SWEEPSTAKES ENTRY FORM

Complete and return this Entry Form immediately—the more Entry Forms you submit, the better your chances of winning!
- Entry Forms must be received by **December 31, 1990**
- A random draw will take place on **January 29, 1991**   3-HT-1-SW
- Trip must be taken by **December 31, 1991**

YES, I want to win a PASSPORT TO ROMANCE vacation for two! I understand the prize includes round-trip air fare, accommodation and a daily spending allowance,

Name_____

Address_____

City_____ State_____ Zip_____

Telephone Number_____ Age_____

Return entries to: **PASSPORT TO ROMANCE**, P.O. Box 9056, Buffalo, NY 14269-9056

COUPON BOOKLET/OFFER CERTIFICATE

Item	LEVEL ONE Booklet 1	LEVEL TWO Booklet 1 & 2	LEVEL THREE Booklet 1, 2 & 3	LEVEL FOUR Booklet 1, 2, 3 & 4
Booklet 1 = $100+	$100+	$100+	$100+	$100+
Booklet 2 = $200+		$200+	$200+	$200+
Booklet 3 = $300+			$300+	$300+
Booklet 4 = $400+	____	____	____	$400+
Approximate Total Value of Savings	$100+	$300+	$600+	$1,000+
# of Proofs of Purchase Required	4	6	12	18
Check One	____	____	____	____

Name_____

Address_____

City_____ State_____ Zip_____

Return Offer Certificates to: **PASSPORT TO ROMANCE**, P.O. Box 9057, Buffalo, NY 14269-9057

Requests must be postmarked by **January 25, 1991**

✂ -

ONE PROOF OF PURCHASE   3-HT-1

To collect your free coupon booklet you must include the necessary number of proofs-of-purchase with a properly completed Offer Certificate   © 1990 Harlequin Enterprises Limited

See previous page for details